PRAISE

"Like a strange, [...] all those who crack its pages."

—*Vogue*

"I can't believe this is Emily Zhou's debut—it's one of the most well-crafted short story collections I've had the pleasure of reading."

—NPR

"Intimate and perceptive ... comes to life in the details that fill early adulthood for a cast of memorable young queer and trans characters—escape-artist cats, house parties that are equal parts awkward and alluring, and dead-end jobs abided until real life begins."

—*San Francisco Chronicle*

"A fresh and new voice in short fiction ... a strong talent ... [Zhou] has a knack for creating memorable scenes and her stories feel lived in."

—*Toronto Star*

"In the last few years we've been blessed with several stellar entries into the trans woman lit canon, and *Girlfriends* is looking to be the best of the year. A tight short story collection that never overstays its welcome...heartily recommended."

—*Colorado Sun*

"Tender, incisive portraits of trans womanhood, the ties that bind women to one another ... Simultaneously aligned with queer coming-of-age story collections of previous generations and dexterously subverting and revitalizing the genre, these seven stories offer a glimpse into the future of queer literature...this bright writer is leading the way."

—*Kirkus*

"Zhou's vibrant debut collection chronicles the often-messy lives of her young trans women protagonists ... [they] spring to life through dialogue, body postures, and personal style, whether it's facial piercings, flannel, or hoop earrings."

— Publishers Weekly

"Girlfriends is great ... finely observed and funny and, in a way I find a bit difficult to describe, so very queer. Partly this is because they go about various recognizably queer business, but also partly I think because their fears and insecurities and the places they get stuck feel queer in a way it never quite does when straight people write queer characters—Zhou is both a great observer and also, clearly, someone with a clear and practised memory for how it felt to have so many feelings."

—Xtra

"Like people-watching at a particularly eclectic party while your insightful, biting, and painfully self-conscious friend whispers judgment and gossip in your ear."

— Autostraddle

"Girlfriends sounds a loud bell announcing the change of guard: a generational arrival. Here is a writer who can scrap with the likes of Ann Beattie or Richard Ford but attends parties to which those boomers (or for that matter, we millennials) would never get invited."

—Torrey Peters, author of Detransition, Baby

"Beautifully rendered and utterly compelling, Emily Zhou's stories remind me of late night phone conversations with a dear friend—a space that always feels fresh, no matter how many social triumphs and dysfunctions are nursed and examined—and where despite impossible ambiguities and distances, love strikes."

—Dodie Bellamy, author of The Letters of Mina Harker

"Reading these pages immersed me in the slow transformative thrill of refusal. Emily Zhou knows how to arrive at an ending. Her stories capture the particular texture of those moments in which we turn away, not yet knowing what we are turning towards, but certain that whatever habits and attitudes we've become used to are over."

—H Felix Chau Bradley, author of *Personal Attention Roleplay*

"Emily Zhou is a writer that doesn't let you take sides. In these exquisite and discomforting stories characters talk at eachother and rarely say what they really feel while their body language and their bodies find a way to make t hemselves heard. *Girlfriends* is untidy, hilarious, heart-breaking, and always satisfying. Zhou is a true witness. This is the fiction we've been waiting for."

— Corinne Manning, author of *We Had No Rules*

"Soaked in melancholy and the easy rhythm of café hangs, ad-hoc photoshoots, and cutting remarks, these sharply observed stories navigate identities, fraying relationships, and the parties and mores of today's transsexual demimonde. Here Emily Zhou comes fully into her own terrifying powers: a writer to watch, just as she's watching all of us."

—Jeanne Thornton, author of *Summer Fun*

"An absolute triumph! I had to force myself not to tear through it ... I was completely amazed by Zhou's ability to not only conjure a whole world out of small encounters, asides, and individual experiences but also to render the most weighty and resonant story approachable without diminishing the beating heart and raw emotion at the centre ... super-intimate, beautifully chaotic in places — defiantly unafraid of glorious messiness."

—John Toews, McNally Robinson Booksellers (Winnipeg, MB)

"Her stories of trans girls' relationships (to each other, to cis queers, to men) are tender, realized portraits of young womanhood. I read this book in a day and can't wait to shove it into the hands of our store's patrons."

— Charlie Jones, A Room of One's Own Bookstore (Madison, WI)

"What an incredible read. Seven glittering stories with such beautiful clarity and perspective. Reminds me a ton of Beattie's mid to late career. I will absolutely be reading anything and everything Emily Zhou writes from now on."

— Matthew Montgomery, McNally Robinson Booksellers (Winnipeg, MB)

"Compelling…vibrant, rich… she brings seven startlingly authentic voices to life … [Girlfriends] is a phenomenal debut."

— Michigan Daily

GIRLFRIENDS

EMILY ZHOU

Copyright © 2023 by Emily Zhou

All rights reserved. No part of this book may be reproduced in any part by any means — graphic, electronic, or mechanical — without the prior written permission of the publisher, except by a reviewer, who may use brief excerpts in a review.

Published by LittlePuss Press, Brooklyn, NY
littlepuss.net

This is a work of fiction. Any resemblance of characters to persons either living or deceased is purely coincidental.

A version of "Affection" was previously published in *Joyland*, 2023.

Cover image by Liu Xiaodong
Three Transsexuals, 2001
200x200cm Oil on Canvas
© Liu Xiaodong, Courtesy of Lisson Gallery

Cover design by Zoe Norvell
Edited by Casey Plett
Proofread by Veronica Esposito

Printed and bound in the United States
on FSC®-certifed paperstock

MIX
Paper | Supporting responsible forestry
FSC® C005010

ISBN 978-1-7367168-4-7 (print)
ISBN 978-1-7367168-5-4 (e-book)

3 5 7 9 10 8 6 4

Table of Contents

Affection	3
Performance	19
Means to an End	51
Separate Ways	77
Do-over	91
Ponytail	117
Gap Year	133

girlfriends

Emily Zhou

Affection

After Sylvie found out that Marina was dropping out of graduate school, she sent her a long, philosophical email that ended with an invitation to her new girlfriend's housewarming party at the end of the week, with the implication that they'd talk it all out there.

Marina didn't respond to the email. Sylvie used to send her links to Instagram flyers for events around campus: mixers for grad students in the humanities, a "queer and trans clothing swap" at the one gay bar, themed happy hours. This was just like that, exactly like that.

On Friday, she got back from work and realized that she would, despite herself, regret it if she didn't go. It was better than nothing, and nothing else was going on, and she knew barely anyone else in this town. Wading into her barely unpacked bedroom, she found her one good dress and some lipstick in the bottom of a suitcase, gritted her teeth as she made herself pretty while leaning over the bathroom sink.

An hour later she got off the bus on the other side of town and followed the map on her phone to a short, dead-end street. The sun had just slipped out of sight. In the few lit windows in the suburban bungalows, couples watched TV and families ate dinner. Light and the smell of smoke came from the backyard of the house on the corner, hidden by a tall wooden fence. She took slow steps down the street, examining each house, before arriving at a big, tall Victorian mansion at the end of the street.

She double-checked the address and then stood there, disbelieving, until a pair of men came around the mansion from the side yard and walked past her, seeming not to notice. She went on standing there. When they were almost out of sight, one of them turned around and called out, "it's around back, honey."

She opened the gate and shuffled cautiously around the house. Sure enough, just behind the side yard there was a lower building with a separate driveway — an old, two-story carriage house under the shadow of a few big, twisted trees. Purple light and electronic music came out of the windows. The heavy double doors on one side were flung open and small groups of people stood in the gravel in front of them. Marina walked past them without saying a word and stood in the entryway.

Inside was one long room with a kitchen at one end. A couple dozen people — young, queerish, wearing flannels and jeans or big skirts and hoop earrings — milled around, sitting on each other's laps or leaning against walls, gesturing with drinks in their hands, drifting around, never alone. No one seemed to pay much attention to her as she stood there, chewing on the end of a strand of hair and looking around the room for anyone she knew. Watching the motion of the crowd, a familiar feeling of immobility settled in her. She willed herself to take a step forward, then another one.

She spotted Sylvie on the other side of the room, on a couch draped over her girlfriend, Perrin, who was spindly and had a lot of facial piercings. When Marina shuffled over, the two disentangled and Sylvie gave her a brief hug, her hands only just touching Marina's shoulders before drawing away. Perrin nodded and smiled at her.

"We have to talk," Sylvie said to Marina, shouting to be heard. "I'm sure I'll run into you. I want to give it a good chunk of time. Maybe outside." With that, she kissed Perrin on the back of her neck and rose from the couch. After a moment, Perrin got up and followed her.

Marina took their spot and looked around. After a minute or two of feeling very outside of the scene, with everyone talking loudly and touching each other, Marina politely asked the boy next to her for a hit of the orange bong he was smoking. He wordlessly handed it to her. She inhaled too hard, coughed, and then couldn't stop coughing. People looked over at her from their conversations.

"Water's in the kitchen, babe," the boy next to her said, looking sympathetically at her.

She got up and caught her breath in front of the sink, drank two glasses of water, then realized that she was already alarmingly high, to the point that talking to someone would be complicated. For a moment she sank into the pleasurable sensation, her whole body floating away from where she stood on the surface of the earth, then she felt the resignation, the muteness, come back. It faintly occurred to her that Sylvie could have introduced her to the rest of the circle. Maybe Sylvie had given up on her too.

She sat back down and tried to just let her mind rest neutrally on the scene in front of her. *At least I'm here*, she thought. And then: *How hard can it be to just sit there and wait for something to happen?*

She found that she could calm herself, prevent everything from floating away, by focusing on the body language of the people right in front of her: two gay-looking guys and one vaguely nonbinary-looking person with an undercut wearing a silver jumpsuit. She didn't stare but let her eyes sort of drift over the trio as they moved their hands, drank from red plastic cups, adjusted their bodies.

"I said, what's your name?"

She blinked. The silver jumpsuit person was looking at her.

"Marina."

Silver Jumpsuit leaned in and widened their eyes. "Oh, you're Sylvie's friend! The writer."

"Uh, yeah."

"What do you write?" said one of the gay guys. The other one had run off. Marina got a fresh look at him and noticed that he was very attractive. Her eyes ascended from his hands up his long, thin arms fluted with muscle and spotted with freckles, to his shoulders, bare in a black tank top. There were little red flowers embroidered on the thin strip of fabric that covered his collarbones. He had a face as square as a Roman statue and a nest of brownish curls that got in his eyes.

"Poetry," Marina said.

(Was it possible that he would be into girls? Maybe she wasn't, like, girl enough yet for him to be, like, categorically uninterested? It's not like in a sane world her *pronouns* would be a determining factor there. She let herself fall into that hypothetical. She *was* wearing a dress, and had long hair that was up in a braided bun, but, well, that was about all. But then she had the thought that men and women are beautiful in different ways, and it's not like your credits transfer over.)

"What kind of poetry?" he said.

"I mean, I — I'm not really writing. I mean, I'm not really writing anything right now, but I did write poetry before. Sorry, I'm really high and I didn't get your name. Either of your names."

He laughed and held out his hand. She felt what she imagined to be an electric charge go up her forearm as his fingers curled under her hand.

"Nico."

"He's Nicki sometimes," Silver Jumpsuit said.

"Not right now," he said, smiling as if embarrassed.

"I'm Marina. Full-time," Marina said.

Silver Jumpsuit nodded. "I'm Aubrey, they/them/theirs."

Marina nodded back. "Um, how do you two know Perrin?"

"I work with her at the gallery," Nico said.

"I show my work there a lot," Aubrey said. Their voice had shades of vocal fry around the edges. "I'm a photographer, and Nico and Perrin are basically the only actual gallerists in this town that show, like, art that takes *risks* right now."

"Cool," Marina said, unsure what the expected response was.

"I think I want to smoke a cigarette," Nico announced.

"Yeah, I'll come with," Aubrey said.

He seemed bored. Marina looked at him again. "Me too," she said.

≈

They went upstairs to a dim hallway and out to the roof through Perrin's bedroom.

"Finally," Aubrey breathed into the hot night air. "Ugh. A moment of *calm*."

"Amen to that," Nico said, sitting on the sloped tiles and looking out into the deserted street. Before long they were talking about something incomprehensible to Marina. He handed her his lighter. She lay on her back and watched an airplane passing between mackerel clouds way up there, all her being focused on its flickering track.

Gradually, Aubrey's conversation with Nico dried up. They turned to Marina. "So, like, what do you do now," they asked, "if you used to be a poet?"

"I think I'm still a poet," Marina said, not sitting up. "I haven't forgotten how to do it."

"That's real," Aubrey said.

"Is the Nicki thing like your drag queen persona?" Marina asked, turning her head to Nico.

"Yeah, from back when I lived in Chicago," he said. "It's sort of becoming its own thing, though."

"Oh," Marina said.

When the silence seemed to stretch out, she asked Aubrey if she could see their photographs. Aubrey obligingly pulled up their artist website on their phone.

The pictures were arranged in a grid that moved when Marina swiped at the screen with her index finger. Black-and-white pictures of parts of naked bodies, zoomed in to closer-than-intimate distances, to an abstracting closeness that rendered body parts as collections of shapes. A hand grabbed a thigh covered in flower tattoos, a hand held a knife flat to a torso, another hand held a mouth open, the rest of the head out of view. In most of them, she couldn't discern the number or gender of their subjects, for all the overlapping limbs and indistinct layers of fabric covering and revealing by turns.

"Wow, these are — intense," Marina said, flicking through the grid faster.

"That's the word everyone uses," Aubrey said with evident satisfaction.

"It's hard to describe their stuff, right?" Nico said. "Like, I dunno, so much art about bodies is so boring, or self-congratulating, like the artist expects a gold star for showing people doing uncomfortable things or even just for *displaying* the body. Aub is more interesting than that."

"Definitely," Marina said.

When she looked up from the phone at Nico, she was surprised again by his beauty and looked back down, unseeing, at Aubrey's art, to disguise her eyes.

"Definitely," Marina said again. She gestured with her hands and continued: "The, um, scenarios that these people are in seem kind of dangerous, or aggressive, almost? But there's this sense of affection there, even if you don't get to see the whole person. Or, like, the fact that you don't get to see the whole person, but you get to see their sense of affection, even if that affection is dangerous — you know?"

Aubrey smiled. "Yeah, exactly," they said.

"Can you guess which ones are me?" Nico said.

Marina looked back at the phone. She picked one at random and looked between him and the phone. It was a photograph of someone's hairy, skinny torso with four female-looking hands palming it. He looked back at her with an expectant face, and she locked eyes with him for a moment.

"No," she said, and Aubrey laughed.

"One time when they had an opening it was full of our friends pointing at the wall and going, 'that's me!'" Nico said. "They bring the camera everywhere. I bet they have it tonight."

"Do you?" Marina said.

"Oh, yeah," Aubrey said, smiling and not looking at her. "I take a lot of pictures at parties just for, like, myself, Instagram, you know. I don't do it that much anymore, but, y'know, I like to have the option."

"We could get more drunk and take pictures of each other," Nico said.

"Sure," Aubrey said. "I'm not taking it out here, though, and I don't really feel like taking it out downstairs; it's like, as soon as I take that thing out everybody is suddenly not being themselves, they're *acting*. I bet Perrin would be fine with us using her bedroom."

They crawled through the window and Nico sprawled out on Perrin's bed, his arms splayed behind him. The room was small and neat — museum postcards pinned to the walls, an incense burner next to a jewelry rack and a little makeup mirror on the dresser, cream-colored bedding. Nico reached behind the bedposts and found a switch for some red LED lights that snaked around the top of the walls.

"Cute," Aubrey said approvingly as the room turned a deep, computer red. "Maybe I'll keep the color in these for the first time in forever. Grey to red. Probably not though. Keep those on, I like that kinda dim light."

They finished attaching the lens to the camera and pointed it from across the room at Nico, who smiled a coy smile at it. Marina watched Aubrey get progressively closer to Nico's face with the camera lens until it was almost right up against it. Nico covered parts of his face with his hands and giggled while Aubrey snapped pictures. Eventually he grabbed the camera out of their hands with a single graceful gesture and took one with the flash on right in Aubrey's face when they tried to take it back from him.

"Oh fuck you," Aubrey said, laughing. "Here, you two can amuse yourselves with that thing, I'll be back. If you break it you owe me six hundred dollars."

I get it, Marina thought. *This is fun. It's a game.*

"Honestly, when you suggested this I was worried I'd have to get naked like everyone in those photographs," Marina said once Aubrey was gone. She sat on the floor facing Nico, who was still sitting on the bed.

"I mean, we could," he said.

"Display the body," Marina quoted, imitating Nico's lisp.

"It's kind of bullshit but you have to believe in it for it to work," Nico said, aiming the camera lens at her. She instinctively started to cover her face, and then something in her made her drop her hands and stare head-on at the device. She had no idea what facial expression she was making. He snapped the shutter and the flash went off, blinding her.

"What's bullshit?" she said, blinking. "Getting naked for art?"

"Yeah," he said. "And just, like, in general. You have to suspend doubt."

"I feel like you're asking me to take off my clothes," Marina said recklessly.

"Knock yourself out, girl," Nico said, taking another picture, with the flash off this time.

"Sure," Marina said, and before she could think she had undone her bra and taken off her dowdy shirt dress. "Let's do some nudes."

He laughed. "Okay, fine. I'm no Aubrey, but I'll try."

They traded places, Nico on the floor and Marina standing next to the bed, the LED lights coloring her bare skin a deep mauve. Neither moved for a moment. The only solution to this situation was to move, she thought, and she was immobile.

She experimentally covered her mouth with the back of her forearm and Nico clicked the shutter once. She dropped her hand; he clicked the shutter again. Marina sat heavily on the bed, crossed and uncrossed her legs, cracked her neck, undid the swirly knot at the top of her head and heard the small clattering of her hairpins bouncing off the wooden floor as her hair cascaded down the side of her face. She arched her back so that her rib cage protruded and her breasts disappeared, she craned her head way to the side. *Click click click.* He kept looking up and over the camera body at her, smiling. She smiled back, came close to laughing a few times but kept herself in check. It took some practice to not flinch at the snap of the mechanism.

"Okay, okay," she said finally. It could have been five minutes or an hour. She waved her hand at him and then lay down on the bed so she wouldn't have to look at the lens anymore. He snapped one last picture of her laying there in her panties and then walked over to the bed and lay down next to her.

"I feel like some of those are gonna turn out good," he said. He was scrolling through something on his phone with one hand.

"Yeah, maybe," Marina said.

"You wanna take some of me?" he said.

"No," she said. She was suddenly tired of all of this and wanted to go home again, but she tried to sound simply disinterested. "Okay, here, I'll do one," she said. She turned on her side and propped her elbow on the bed. She took the camera from him and took a picture of him looking at his phone. He turned to look at her, and they were both laying there.

The door opened.

"I need to take back the expensive thing I use to make my art," Aubrey announced. "Sorry. Oh, Marina, you're naked, that's cool."

The shame hit her belatedly and she tried to cover her body with Perrin's blankets.

"I took some nudes of her," Nico said, still looking at whatever was on his phone.

"Oh, lemme see," Aubrey said, taking the camera back from Marina. "Oh, I love this one," they said, looking into the little screen. "Yeah, I can edit these and send them to you?"

"Sure," Marina said. She was sure she was red in the face.

"I really like these," Aubrey said. Nico and Marina both looked intently at them as they pressed buttons on the back of the camera. Then they looked up at the two of them, seemed to think, and cautiously raised the camera and took a picture of the two of them sitting side by side on the bed.

"Sorry, I should have asked," Aubrey said, lowering the camera. "But you two just look, like, so good next to each other."

"I bet," Marina said.

"We could do some together," Nico said.

"Yeah? How does that sound, Marina?" Aubrey said.

"Sure," Marina said before she could get herself to think better of it. It seemed like a good way to remain with Nico, even if she had already resigned herself to her feeling that he was probably not interested at all.

"Yay," Aubrey said softly, already fiddling with the camera settings.

"That means Nico has to take off his clothes too," Marina added.

"It's only fair," he said, taking off his shirt. "Feminist, even." He turned to her. "Ready?"

"Yeah," Marina said, her voice coming out breathy and sustained as she looked at him shamelessly. He didn't seem to notice.

"How should we start?" Nico asked, looking at Aubrey.

"Hmm, maybe Marina, you could stand on the bed and Nico, lie down? Yeah, like — oh, maybe you could put one foot on either side of his legs, and sort of let your hair — yes, exactly."

There she was, awkwardly looking down at him. She thought she was shivering and wondered if either of them would notice, if the camera would pick up some residue from her trembling body. She closed her eyes and reached down with both hands for him, bent her knees, almost fell toward him. Aubrey clicked the shutter.

Aubrey never stopped moving, finding new ways to aim and point the lens. Every so often, they would say, almost embarrassed, some command to the two of them, and the two of them would reposition their bodies. Aubrey had them hug, had Nico cover Marina's face with his hands, had Marina place her hands on his chest, his waist, his thighs. The first few touches had the same electric charge as before, but gradually it faded. Eventually, Aubrey stopped issuing commands and the two of them just moved on their own, touching each other experimentally, almost without emotion.

"You guys are great at this," Aubrey said admiringly. Marina turned and saw that they weren't taking any more pictures. "God, just looking at the raw images here — I really think most of those are gonna be really good."

"I hope you got one of that moment with all that hand-face stuff," Nico said, sounding amused. "I feel like some of those are gonna be really weird. You have to send us these when they're done."

"Yeah, totally," Aubrey said, tossing Nico's t-shirt and Marina's dress and bra back onto the bed. Nico sat up and slipped the shirt on in one elegant movement. Marina remained lying facedown. Her head was spinning again.

"Cool. I'm leaving, Nicki. I'm kinda wired, so maybe I'll edit these tonight."

"Bye Aub," Nico said, not looking up.

"Wanna go back out on the roof?" Marina said, after the door closed and she had started buttoning her dress.

"You read my mind," Nico said.

≈

He wordlessly handed her his jacket and they climbed back through the window. The night air had become colder and she was suddenly herself again, and Nico was just Nico, a pretty stranger. There had been a moment where it seemed like — whatever.

Across the street, lights were on. Her eyes lingered on an arched window covered with a thin lace curtain. Through it, she could see the shadowy outline of a person behind a laptop and the vague shapes of furniture. They made small talk. She asked him questions about the gallery and about the art world, and he rambled digressively. At one point he put his arm around her shoulders and she leaned ever so slightly, felt his protruding ribs nudge against hers.

"You're nice," she said drowsily into his shoulder. He was midsentence and cut himself off and sort of awkwardly stroked her other shoulder, bare and exposed to the cold night air where it was slipping out of the dress, which she had put back on hastily.

He stubbed out his cigarette and tossed it over the edge into the empty street. "I'm cold," he said abruptly. "Want to go back in?"

The anticipation was so thick it was like her whole body was vibrating. When they climbed back into the window they immediately kissed, and he fell back onto the bed and pulled her on top of him, he was fumbling with the buttons on her dress, grabbing her thighs. Marina giggled and pulled gently on his hair so she could kiss his neck, and then his collarbone. A warm, fluttery sensation spread through her body as she let her hair cover his face like a curtain. She didn't even mind when he reached under the hem of her dress and grabbed her dick. She closed her eyes and kissed him harder and considered the sensation for a moment before climbing off him and undoing the fly of his jeans.

This was what she wanted. She drew her tongue, and then her whole mouth, across the taut skin of his glans, then opened her jaw as wide as it would go to take in the rest of it. He whimpered a little bit and pushed her head a little further toward his pelvis with his surprisingly strong hand. Her eyes rolled back into her head.

Before anything else could happen, someone knocked on the door. Both of them jumped back from each other at the sound.

"It's Aubrey. I think I left my phone in there."

"Also Perrin," Perrin's voice said through the door.

She leaned over and kissed him again.

"We should probably get out of this room," she said into his ear.

"Probably," he said without moving.

She loved that he was more embarrassed than she was. They walked past Perrin and Aubrey without saying a word. "It's fine, I just wish you had asked first," Marina heard Perrin saying.

They were back in the big room, next to the kitchen. For a moment they avoided looking at each other, and then Marina reached out and placed her hand on his shoulder.

"You're sweet, Nicki," she said.

"You're sweet too," he said, still not looking at her. All around them people were talking loudly to each other, touching each other.

"I feel like we kinda fucked up," he said, taking a step back.

"Uh-huh."

"I should probably apologize to Perrin."

"Yeah, probably," she said. "I hope Aubrey edits those pictures. I really want to see them."

"They will," he said, and then he walked away in the direction of the rest of the party. Marina looked for Sylvie again, and then left.

～

When she got home, it was still early. She sat in her chair by the window and drank half a bottle of wine too quickly and barely made it into bed before falling asleep.

The next morning when she checked her phone, she saw that Aubrey had added her and Nico to a group chat with the photos. Marina looked at them while still under the covers. At least she had his number now.

Aubrey sent over maybe a dozen pictures. Within a few minutes, Marina had decided which ones she liked and which she didn't, downloaded the ones she liked, and begun to look at only those over and over.

There it was, her body, her face. She imagined these on a gallery wall, like Nico had said.

There had been trans muses in art history, and she thought about them while she took a long shower, using up all the hot water, trying unsuccessfully to dispel the headache that had been forming behind her eyes. That whole Warhol thing. Were they ashamed too?

Nico texted the group chat: *these are great*

Aubrey texted: *i really like them. marina you're so pretty, was v nice meeting you last night*

Marina responded: *yeah thanks for these! it was nice meeting you both*

Sylvie had also texted her: *per's kinda mad about you and miss nico fucking in her bed. don't worry about it though. didn't think he liked girls at all*

Marina responded: *god should i apologize? hard to say what happened there. im still sorting it out*

Sylvie responded: *couldn't hurt, I mean nico did, yall didn't do anal right? she was worried about that*

Marina didn't respond, instead drafting a series of elaborate texts to Nico in her head as she made herself eggs and toast and coffee. She ate it standing up in the kitchen, staring out the window into her backyard.

After doing her breakfast dishes she texted him:

hey!

last night was nice :) id love to see you again

could be coffee, a walk, breakfast, whatever

It was a Saturday, and although the morning was mostly over, the amount of time that stretched out in front of her seemed obscene. She tried reading and tidied her room and took a walk in the bracing sunlight through sidewalks filled with leaves. When she got back, she had a missed call from Sylvie, and when she called her back, Sylvie told her that Perrin wasn't mad anymore, and also, was she free tomorrow morning for brunch?

So that was all right. After she reheated herself leftovers, Nico texted her back:

hey! sorry for the delay lol

you're coming to brunch tmrw right? w perrin? sylvie told me u were. aub will be there for sure

apparently per was super mad lol. but it's fin now

*fine

we should walk/talk afterward

Marina's stomach fluttered. She thought about how easy touching him had been.

She responded *yes please* and turned her phone off. For the rest of the day, she didn't think about him at all as she took clothes out of suitcases and put them into the wardrobe and dresser. She turned her phone back on a few hours later just to look at the pictures.

She stared at them, memorizing the angles her limbs were taking. Her facial expression balanced between defiant and receptive; the half-smile she had in a few of them. She remembered Nico was making that same facial expression as he looked at her from over the camera body.

Later, in the mirror as she was washing her face, she looked up from the basin and stared at her reflection in the bright bathroom light, and kept staring until the soap got in her eyes.

Performance

"Was he ugly?"

Lara straightened her back and looked at Tess across the small, round table. She seemed to be deciding what to say.

"No," Lara said. "He was fine. I'm like, not into men like that, but y'know — it could be worse."

"Sure," Tess said.

"He's got a beard, glasses. He looks like Professor Harrison."

Tess looked down at the table into her half-full, tepid cappuccino, then back up at Lara. Around them in the midday coffee shop, people their age were looking into their laptops or hunched over binders full of papers.

"How much is he paying you?" Tess said.

"Six hundred," Lara said. "Three times what I used to get from camming in a week. He said he's lonely, he hates his job, can't get laid, and doesn't want to bother trying anymore, wants to stay inside with his books, so he'll want to see me like, once, twice a month."

"You have, like, pepper spray, right?" Tess said, lowering her voice.

"Yeah," Lara said, not lowering hers at all. "And a knife. If he tries anything, he's gonna lose an eye or something."

"Okay, good," Tess said.

"I'm not worried," Lara said. "He's as gentle as a *lamb*."

Tess wrinkled her nose.

"Sure," she said. "But, you know, I'm worried about you."

"Don't be," Lara said. "I think this is gonna be fine. Less time-intensive than camming."

Tess looked back down at her cappuccino, realizing she wasn't going to finish it. In the two years they had known each other, it seemed to Tess that Lara had never once noticed the anxious, motherly attachment Tess had for her. In fact Lara had been aware of it from the start.

"What did you tell him your name is again?"

"Kitty," Lara said. "He didn't like that, so I told him it's short for Katie."

"Katie," Tess said slowly.

"It's, like, not my name, but I could see it," Lara said.

Tess tilted her head to the side and narrowed her eyes slightly. "Sure," she said.

≈

Lara had chosen her name before and it was weird to pick another one, even though (or maybe because) it was a similar process. She had stood in her room and stared at herself in the mirror while she wore the clothes the name would live in. After a while, the name — diminutive, emptied of personality, *available* — presented itself to her spontaneously.

She had misjudged him: It turned out that what he was after was something other than an empty vessel to be filled with his fantasies. On the walk they had taken around the park by the river that she had chosen as a way to make sure he wasn't a serial killer, he had wanted to talk to her about her studies and had gone on and on about Theodore Dreiser, whom he had written his PhD dissertation on nearly a decade prior. His diction was careful if a little pretentious, and he spoke in a quiet, low monotone. At the end of it he had asked if Kitty was her real name and she realized she would have to adjust her persona a bit.

"Yes," Lara said.

"Is that what you go by?" he said. "Among friends, I mean."

"I'm not your friend," she said.

He returned his gaze to the woodchipped path.

"You're right," he said. "I'm sorry."

"If you want to know," Lara said, affecting a conciliatory tone, "my real name is Katie. My friends call me Kitty."

"I guess I should call you Katie, then," he said. "Because I'm not your friend."

"Right," Lara said.

He had this strange way of looking at her. Not possessively, but curiously, and unabashedly. He liked to emphasize a point he was making by turning his head toward her and making eye contact.

She walked him back to his car in the parking lot behind the hospital and watched him drive off. Standing there, she realized how tense she was. It really was like becoming another person. She mouthed her two new names — Kitty, Katie. There was really no way to tell if he was a serial killer or not, she realized.

≈

At night, she ruminated on the meeting with him. There were skills of compartmentalization she would have to learn.

She found herself thinking about one night a year ago, maybe the first time she had realized she was pretty. She had gone early to a party her friend Jenna hosted at her apartment on Thayer Street. Her boyfriend, Kenny, had just returned from an internship on the East Coast; Jenna had just returned from a year abroad in Paris. It was a housewarming party for the apartment they were signing a lease on together.

By the time Lara got there, the apartment was in perfect order, with bottles and cups lined up on the kitchen counter and jazz playing from a small Bluetooth speaker on the granite coffee table. Jenna answered the door.

Jenna was thinner and her dirty blonde hair was longer and streaked with sun. She gave Lara a tight hug.

"Hi you," she said into Lara's shoulder. Then, pulling away, over her shoulder: "Ken, Lara's here. Pour the lady some wine."

Then, directed back at Lara: "You look *amazing*, by the way."

It was true that Lara had made an effort, even beyond the transformation she had effected over the previous year. She had grown out her brownish-auburn hair just above shoulder-length, and she was wearing a black halter-top jumpsuit, a lace choker, and bright red, shiny shit-kicker boots. She had finished with glossy pink lipstick and cat eyes ridged with pink eyeshadow. It made her eyes seem wider and her entire face that much longer. She had learned that trick from a girl on YouTube whose room was bright and white, like a drawing.

Once they had all sat on the couch, Jenna launched into a recap of her last few weeks in Italy and Greece. Kenny wordlessly emerged from the kitchen with a glass of wine, which turned out to be a bright, astringent retsina Jenna had brought back with her.

Jenna had gone from a mousy girl with huge glasses to one of the most self-possessed women Lara had ever met, but Kenny had stayed the same. He was tall, somewhat plump, with stubble and glasses, an unsure body language, and a facial expression that suggested a perpetual mild confusion. Most likely, Lara thought, she used to be like that too.

"I managed to avoid all the other Americans," Jenna was saying with evident satisfaction. "While they were all on planes back to the Midwest, I was in Rome speaking French. Like, *really* speaking it."

Kenny met Lara's eye and gave her a wry smile that Lara returned.

"Anyway, I won't bore you," Jenna said. "He's already sick of all the Europe talk."

"It's more interesting than Baltimore," Kenny said meekly.

"Neither of us have heard about *you*," Jenna said to Lara.

"Well, I've been okay," Lara said gingerly. "I declared the English major, finally."

Jenna nodded. Kenny shifted in his seat a bit and looked at Lara, who shrugged.

"That's about all that's new with me. Besides, you know — "

"Sure," Kenny said.

They covered the usual start-of-semester topics — the finding of the apartments, the course load, the new research interests — and after this had been exhausted, Jenna went back to talking about Paris, which she clearly had left only in body. For maybe twenty, thirty minutes, Kenny or Lara didn't interrupt. One story would lead right into the next one. A lot of her stories involved a clique of French boys in her classics module who would take her out on their mopeds and smoke cigarettes with her on bridges and rooftops. She often mentioned Jean-Claude, a former gymnast who studied dialects of Latin. When Jenna brought up the French girls in her program, it was usually to indicate how stuck-up they were or how they inexplicably didn't like her, and she only mentioned the other Americans with open derision. They didn't understand Europe, she said, they brought America with them, they weren't willing to try living differently.

There was a story that went on for quite a while about Jean-Claude rescuing her from a miscommunicated Uber destination and an overeager acquaintance who worked in publishing. Lara looked over at Kenny and noticed that he was staring down at the carpet. Was it possible he hadn't heard about all of this, or that he hadn't put two and two together? They had agreed to be "open" for the year prior, so this sort of thing was to be expected. She knew from Jenna's emails that he had slept with a few women and that it had bothered her an appropriate amount and no more, but she could tell from Kenny's face that he hadn't considered that Jenna would, in less than a year, find *this* seemingly charming, sensitive, companionable guy who had furnished so many picturesque anecdotes.

Lara kept waiting for the balance of the conversation to be restored. *Maybe being straight always means compartmentalizing*, she thought; she was only surprised it was to *this* degree.

Fairly zoned out by that point, Lara didn't realize she was staring at Kenny until he turned away from the window and caught her eye. Lara quickly looked away. Then she looked back at him. He was looking at her again. Again, Lara met his eyes and then looked at Jenna, who had moved on to a discussion of a particularly stiff-nosed famous classicist whose seminars she had sat in on.

She studied him studying her. He looked intent, curious. The brow knit slightly, his mouth left slightly open for a beat before he closed it again. He looked like he wanted to ask her a question but couldn't find the words.

It took her a while to realize what should have been obvious — he was checking her out in the boring, unsubtle, chauvinistic way that men do to women, to size them up and, possibly, stimulate later fantasy. His eyes kept darting to her, then back to his drink, then a head turn to Jenna, then to some area of empty space, then back to Lara's unspeaking body that was both new and the same. Lara started to meet his gaze head-on. He lost his tentativeness when it became apparent that Lara didn't mean him any harm, her curiosity hid underneath the steadiness of her gaze.

He smiled slightly. Lara didn't return the smile. He looked away again.

Male attention wasn't new to her — the mostly mocking catcalls and leers had begun immediately after she transitioned. This was a scrambled up form of it, though, hard to parse even on the subtextual frequencies that came easier to her now. What did he *want*? Was this normal? Men valued eye contact in each other, didn't they? *Eye contact and a firm handshake*, Lara's father always reminded her, back when she was still speaking to him.

Jenna eventually got around to asking Lara a few questions, after refilling their wine. They were predictable. *How have classes been? Do people ever say anything? You know about the trans studies course here, right? Right, special topics in women's studies, Professor Cayden Harrington.* Kenny nodded along to her brief answers. When people started showing up, it was a relief.

Jenna had been known since freshman year for her low-key, talky parties attended mostly by other brainy women. She had a social talent that had at some point swept Lara into her orbit, along with a number of other prodigy undergraduates and the odd doctoral candidate.

Lara went to the kitchen and poured the rest of the retsina into her glass. She watched Jenna talking to her collection of early arrivals in the entryway. Kenny was on his phone on the couch. He was such an anomaly in Jenna's life, which was otherwise entirely structured around the relentless pursuit of knowledge. He was practical, majored in electrical engineering, and while he wasn't a philistine he clearly didn't understand the ardor with which born academics could follow an associative trail of references and factoids. At parties like this, he tended to interrupt at just the wrong time.

Tess arrived by the time Jenna had gone out to the fire escape to smoke a cigarette. Kenny was relegated to answering the door and making drinks.

"Hi Lara lady," Tess said, leaning down to kiss her cheek. Tess was already a little drunk. "'Scuse me, I have to go say hello to *le salonnière*."

"You should definitely call her that," Lara said.

Lara expected Tess's presence at these parties — the presence of a loud trans girl with green hair who liked to wear silver chains and sheer fabric — to be a bit of a wild card, but she was in honors comp lit and could expound as well as anyone. It was hard to faze these people.

It was hard to keep their attention too. Tess did fine — she had the right level of confidence and unfeigned enthusiasm. After watching Tess enthusiastically greet everyone, even the ones she saw every week, Lara went to the kitchen and found a bottle of port and a fresh red cup. A short time later, she felt drunk enough to engage in some light intellectual bluffing. Before she could rejoin them, though, Kenny came into the kitchen, blocking her egress.

He smiled at her. She smiled back and propped one arm against the countertop.

"Hey. I need a breather," he said.

"I feel that," Lara said.

"Your friend is very interesting."

"Oh?"

"I don't think she's stopped talking since she got here."

"That sounds like her."

He poured himself some rosé.

"How was Baltimore?" she said.

He didn't meet her eyes, even after he put back the bottle of rosé and straightened his neck. His eyes traveled over her shoulders, to her collarbone that poked out of her dress, the curve of her breasts above her rib cage.

"It was fine," he said. "Boring as hell." He kind of shuffled toward her, closing some distance between them.

"Well, we don't have to talk about that."

"Yeah, I'd rather not," he said. "I like being back."

Lara tried to assume the demeanor of a bored girl. She leaned back against the cabinets and sipped from her glass. He leaned awkwardly against the faux-granite countertop that was a little higher than his waist.

"So how's cohabitation treatin' ya?" she said.

He paused for a moment. Lara pursed her lips a little bit and stared at him down her long nose.

"It's different," he finally said.

"I imagine."

"I went from living in a totally empty apartment, to, you know."

Lara looked at the cabinets and the dishes on the countertop and the people in the other room. "Yeah, totally."

"It's a good thing Jenna knows what she's doing, cause I'm hopeless."

"Sure," Lara said. She took a long drink before continuing. "I've always wondered what that dynamic would be like."

He looked like he wanted to avoid the topic and shrugged. Lara gave him a little conciliatory smile.

"I've never lived with a partner before," she added. "It seems so adult."

"Not even for a few days?"

This was where they were, she thought, resorting to hypotheticals and generalizations with each other. She recalled a time, not too long ago, when she talked to this boy most days.

"Oh, I don't know, I've, like, camped at someone's house for a while," Lara said.

He had assumed a relaxed posture in masculine complement to hers: open shoulders, one arm outstretched all the way, casually, carelessly, the hand trailing off the far edge of the counter.

"This is definitely not camping," he said, smiling as though he had told a joke.

He took an ungainly gulp of wine. *What are we doing here*, she thought. This conversation was beginning to feel like a pretense for the body language they were organizing themselves into. She was surprised at how quickly she'd ended up on the other side of this chasm from Kenny. It felt heady, like he held some key to her present self and was giving it to her slowly with each word.

He looked away from her. "So, when you said *partner* — " he started. She watched him trail off into nothing.

Go ahead, she thought, *I won't finish your fucking sentences*.

"Sorry if this is a weird question, but now that you're — "

"I'm gay," she said. "If that's what you mean."

"Oh, I didn't mean — "

"Don't worry about it," she said. "Hey, Kenny, I'm gonna go talk to Tess."

Lara walked past him and touched his shoulder with her fingertips, held it there for just a little longer than he could ignore, and then drifted into the living room. Tess was on the couch with her arm around a woman's shoulders. Lara settled in next to them.

"Laaara lady. You're working on a thesis, right?" Tess said. "We were just talking about ours."

Lara looked up and saw Kenny, aimlessly milling around. Lara smiled at him and he sat down next to her.

"Oh, yes. I'm doing a thesis, I think," Lara said, ignoring him. "I need to finalize it with my advisor."

"Lara, you didn't tell me you were in Honors," Kenny said from around her.

"What's it about?" Tess's companion said. Tess was playing absentmindedly with the other woman's wiry black hair.

"It's about performativity as it relates to two novels by Henry James," Lara said. She finished the wine in her cup, tossing her head back to get the last drops.

"Gotcha," the other woman said.

"You told me about this," Tess said. Then, addressing Kenny: "Lara's pretending to be a feminist theorist, you see. She's gonna figure out what it means to be a woman once and for all."

"Oh, got it," Kenny said, not getting the joke.

"I promise I'm not doing that," Lara said.

"Soon enough Lara's gonna be writing an essay about, like, *Paris Is Burning*."

"What's that?" Kenny said.

"Nothing," Lara said.

"Lara's gonna be like, 'as it turns out, gender is all fake. We know this because of trannies,'" Tess said.

Lara elbowed Tess in the ribs.

"I mean, isn't gender kind of fake?" Kenny said.

Tess and her companion exchanged looks.

"Sorry if that was insensitive," Kenny said.

"No," Lara said. "That's not a bad starting position. But also, 'fake' doesn't mean, like, not real."

"So being trans is like, making the fakeness real?" Kenny said.

"No," Lara said. "The point is that *everyone* is making the fakeness real, all the time."

"Oh," Kenny said.

"I'm not explaining this well, I think," Lara said.

"You're not," Tess said.

"That's fine," Kenny said. "I'm just curious."

"I mean, like, okay," Tess said, dropping the bit. "Gender is, on some level, just performance, because we all do things to indicate to the world that we are the gender we are. The existence of trans people — people who perform gender in, like, 'wrong' or 'marked' ways — are a way for people to say gender is *only* performance. But it's a really cheap way to do it, because it ends up letting cis people off the hook, even if it's meant to call the whole system into question."

"Guys, I'm not even writing about trans people," Lara said.

"Well, you're using the same theoretical tools that lead to these conclusions," Tess said.

"What do you mean by performance, then?" Kenny asked. "Is it just what people do when they're not alone?"

"I'm writing about the ways in which an upper-class woman is gendered differently than a middle-class one," Lara said. "It's not that complicated."

"Oh, got it," Kenny said.

Lara suddenly noticed his proximity — his knee pressed against her thigh, him leaning forward at her, almost close enough for her to see his pores. She felt a wave of revulsion and stood up abruptly. Tess's companion flinched.

"I'll be right back," Lara said.

When she got back from the bathroom, Kenny was gone. Tess looked inquiringly at her. Her companion was resting her head on her shoulder.

"Let's get out of here," Lara said.

Tess seemed in the middle of something, but she was generally pretty good about this sort of thing. When they were outside, Lara felt weightless, like she could float away, join the dry leaves from the neighborhood trees in their wild dance over the pavement.

"So it was that guy, right?" Tess said.

"Yeah. He was giving me vibes."

Lara walked a few steps in front of Tess and pinwheeled her arms in front of her, relishing the vertigo of her intoxication.

"Didn't you know him before you transitioned?" Tess said.

"Yeah."

"Is that weird?"

"I didn't think it was."

"How about now?"

"I don't know," Lara said. "He was just giving me vibes."

Tess caught up to Lara and put both hands on her shoulders.

"C'mon babe. You'll fall."

"I'm *fine*," Lara said.

"How do you feel?" Tess said after a minute or so of silence.

"Like I overreacted," Lara said simply.

"I don't know, I mean — don't gaslight yourself."

"I'm not," Lara said. "I think I'm just unused to that sort of attention."

"He knows you're gay, right?"

"*Yes*," Lara said. "Men are, like, famously *soooo* good at respecting that."

Lara was aware that she wasn't walking in a straight line, and after a few steps she emphasized it, walking in wide, sinusoidal loops down the wide sidewalks.

"Hmm," Tess said.

"H*mm*," Lara mimicked.

"Forget it."

"Forget *what*?" Lara said. "Tell me what you're going to say."

"Okay, fine: I think your beauty makes you feel invincible," Tess said.

"What's *that* supposed to mean?" Lara whined.

"It means you're still trans."

"D*uh* I'm still trans," Lara said. "I don't know what I could have done to make that situation go differently," she continued. "He like, fuckin', *insinuated* himself. And it wasn't even that bad. I'm just not *used* to guys being so obviously *into* me like that."

"Were you into him?"

"Sorta? I was into it, but not him."

"You shouldn't lead people on like that," Tess said. "That, like, could get dangerous, you know?"

She caught up to Lara and grabbed her by the shoulders again. Lara grinned a big drunk grin in Tess's face.

"You sound like a man-hating lesbian," Lara said.

"You know what, forget it."

They talked about something else the rest of the way home. At one point, they stopped so Lara could throw up in the bushes in front of the Episcopal church, the one that had a rainbow flag in the front window.

"God, you're a cheap date," Tess said, holding Lara's hair back. "You had what, three glasses of wine?"

"Fuck you," Lara said, still bent over.

≈

During the subsequent year, male attention never gave Lara the vertigo that Kenny had induced. She acquired the ability to convey, through hints and suggestions, a totalizing *no, thank you* that never failed her.

When she got fired from her library job, she realized that she could start camming and did that for a few months. She hated the lewd messages and initially disappointing amount of money she received, but it led her to Aaron, who sent a polite, solicitous DM one day to her camming profile and a "tip" of two hundred dollars.

Against her better judgment, she replied, and after a short exchange he volunteered that he lived on the north side of Ann Arbor.

I wish I could meet you, he said. *I think you're the most beautiful girl in the world.*

I'm a student at Michigan, Lara responded. *I could meet you. I'm probably half your age or younger. It would cost you, though.*

Naturally, he said.

He seemed to actually understand the parameters of the situation, and the initial meeting had confirmed that he was probably mostly fine. And, you know, that he had cash to burn.

The day before their first appointment, Tess said, "I'd like to talk you out of this."

"Do you have six hundred dollars for me?" Lara said.

"Did you even *try* to get a real job?"

"This is a real job," Lara said.

She affected nonchalance to Tess, the only one who knew about this, but she found herself shaking on the way to the appointment. Her need for six hundred dollars had been momentarily eclipsed by the strangeness of this situation. She was a prostitute, just like that. Somehow she had assumed it would have more intermediary stages. All it required was an encrypted text messaging app and some good luck. When she got off the bus, she took a couple pulls from a flask of whisky that she had stashed in her bag.

His house on the north side was identical in design to the surrounding ones — brick, one floor, four windows in front. When he answered the door, he was wearing a collared shirt under a quarter-zip.

"Hi Katie," he said. "Come on in."

Lara felt like she was about to explode but she made herself take a step forward, then another, then he shut the door behind them. Lara winced.

"I just made some tea," he said. "Come sit with me."

The gray daylight didn't permeate that deeply into the house. Off to one side, there was a living room with upholstered armchairs, couches, a glass-topped coffee table, and an overflowing bookshelf that filled an entire wall, all half in darkness. In the kitchen, there were lace curtains on the windows and a quilted runner down the center of the dining table, a glass-doored cabinet with dusty old plates and photographs. It looked like the house of an old woman. She sat in a chair facing into the kitchen while he poured water into cups.

"So, Katie, how's your semester going?" he said.

"Uh, not too bad," Lara said. "I started my thesis."

"You're studying English, correct?"

"Yeah. I'm doing my thesis on Henry James."

"The Master," he said approvingly, handing her a mug of herbal-smelling liquid and sitting across from her. "That's a worthy subject for someone as bright as you."

He scooted his chair in and placed his elbows on the table.

"Do you know what T.S. Eliot said about James?" Aaron said, sipping his tea. "He said that he had a 'mind so fine no idea could disturb it.' So it's up to us lesser lights to put the ideas back in."

He recited the famous quote ponderously and slowly. Coming out of his mouth, it occurred to Lara for the first time that it was a ridiculous thing to say about a novelist. She could use that, maybe.

"You know this counts as part of your hour, right?" she said.

"Of course," he said. "But it would be sort of artificial to just get right down to it. I thought that we could spend this session just getting to know each other. I'll still pay you."

"I guess you're right," Lara said. She tried to disguise her relief.

"Which novels are you writing about?" he said.

Lara had an elevator pitch ready by this point. "Um, *Portrait* and *Washington Square*. I'm focusing on the characters of Catherine Sloper and Madame Merle. I'm using Butler and Foucault, mostly. Some Bourdieu too, although I mostly disagree with him."

"Mm. When I was your age, no one even thought about reading that Frenchie stuff until graduate school," he said. "Heavy artillery to aim at such delicate artworks. Well, I can sort of imagine your argument there."

Was this a goad, or was the condescension genuine? She propped her elbows on the table and leaned over at him and grinned.

"Tell me what I'm going to say, then," she said.

He leaned back in his seat. His wry smile deepened, revealing laugh lines around his eyes and forehead.

"This is just a guess, but I suppose you mean to say that the characters are products of *discourses*, including but not limited to the discourse of the realist novel, and you're going to endeavor to show that these discourses are essentially male, an unfair game, and in the end you'll have devised a way to extract the morals of the reticent author from his work. The triumph of theory over subjectivity."

"I'm actually going to say that Henry James was a trans woman," Lara said without missing a beat. "And that he hated himself for it so much that he was only capable of producing helpless female dupes and, like, caricatures of manipulative harpies. Both Madame Merle and Cathy Sloper are self-portraits."

"Now that's an interesting thesis," he said.

"I'm joking," Lara said quickly.

"You might not be entirely wrong," he said.

"Don't say that," Lara said.

They both laughed in a forced sort of way. Fifty minutes left, she thought.

≈

Lara kept bringing condoms and a randomly chosen selection from her sex toy drawer each time she went over to Aaron's house, but each time he just wanted to talk. Lara, for the duration of the hour, kept her focus entirely on him, finding ways to keep the conversation going and going.

His house had originally belonged to his mother, a miser who had unexpectedly left him enough money to live off the interest when she died. He mostly read, walked by the river, went out to lunch with a stable of friends around his age. Absent any external motivation to do anything at all, he was "getting a little seedy" as he put it.

In return for his apparent candor, Lara invented a whole alternate past for herself that involved a childhood in California, former troubles with substance abuse, quirky anecdotes about her fake family, hobbies she didn't actually have, and so on.

As months passed — he made appointments to see her every three weeks or so — Lara started to wish that he would make an actual pass at her. It would clarify things. She had signed up to have sex with him for money, she hadn't signed up for whatever this was. The anticipation she felt every time, and its subsequent relief, made her feel slightly crazy in the days following her appointments. She never did anything good with the six hundred each time. It went to expensive clothes, takeout, drugs, books. After a few weeks, she'd be back to doing endless trains of mental math about groceries.

When, in November, she got an email from her old boss at the library, asking if she would want to pick up some shifts, she felt relieved. For a moment she contemplated ghosting Aaron, but no — even if she was getting twice the shifts the library would give her, she would still need his money. So she did both.

One day, close to the end of the semester, Jenna emerged from the stacks with a wild look on her face. She walked right up to Lara's desk and placed both elbows on it.

"Hi Lara," Jenna whispered. "Are you also losing your goddamn mind?"

"Yeah," Lara said.

"When's your shift done? I literally can't think anymore. I need to, like, walk around."

"I get off in an hour. Can you wait that long?"

"No," Jenna said, and walked a few steps away before turning back and mouthing, *Please?*

After checking if her supervisor was there (he wasn't), Lara turned off the light behind the desk and put her coat on. Jenna grinned and they walked out into the freezing night air. When the door closed behind them Jenna let out a prolonged, guttural groan.

"That bad, huh?" Lara said.

"Oh my *god*, he fucking proposed to me."

"Excuse me, *what?*"

"With a *ring*, Lara. His grandmother's fucking *ring*."

"What did you tell him?

"I said I'll think about it."

"That seems reasonable."

"REASONABLE? I'm twenty-one. I can't legally rent a *car*."

Jenna took off her backpack and ran down the library steps, into the snow-covered diag. Lara picked up Jenna's backpack and followed her. The streetlights cast puddles of orange glow in between the bare trees.

"WHAT AM I SUPPOSED TO DO?" Jenna yelled from thirty feet away.

Without really thinking about it, Lara reached down and packed a snowball with her bare hands and lobbed it at Jenna. It fell short. Jenna laughed and threw one back. It hit a tree nowhere near either of them. Lara walked toward her, already feeling her socks getting wet through her boots.

"God, I feel *insane*," Jenna said when Lara was closer.

"I bet," Lara said.

Jenna sat down in the snow, her legs spread wide apart, her unzipped parka billowing around her knees.

"Are you drunk?" Lara asked.

"No. Yes. A little. In my defense, I've been working on this paper for two days straight and now I have this to worry about."

"That's fair."

Lara sat down next to her. Jenna lay down and they looked up at the low, dense winter clouds.

"You know what the paper is about? Jenna said. The 'couple form.' It's like my life is some farce designed to make me crazy."

"What are you saying about it?"

"Oh, that it's — I don't know, if I had to say it without academic jargon I wouldn't be able to believe it."

"What do you believe?" Lara said.

"I BELIEVE — " Jenna yelled up at the sky. She cut herself off. "I *believe* that I have a perfectly good boyfriend who I am in love with, and that I'm not going to marry him."

"When does he want an answer?"

"I'm not giving him an answer. I'm not going to tell him *no*. I'm rejecting the question as out of bounds."

"Can you do that?"

"Yeah," she said. "Why not? He can't just *choose* to make me decide like that."

"That sounds like it means no."

"Maybe. No, yeah, I don't know," Jenna said.

They lay there, in the snow, watching the low clouds billowing above them.

"It's the best I can do," Jenna finally said. "It's the best I can do."

"Sure," Lara said.

≋

"Don't you ever think about changing some of your mom's decorations?" Lara said to Aaron a few days later, back at that dining room table.

"No." He looked around at the heavy curtains and the dusty old furniture. "They suit me just fine."

"Weird, but okay," Lara said. "I have another question for you," she continued. "How do you have the money to see me this often? Is your inheritance really netting you that much?"

He explained he had some online stock trading thing. He did it every day until he made one hundred dollars and then stopped. Then he'd make himself dinner.

"Have you ever lost money?" Lara said.

"Sure," he said. "I usually make it back."

"It's a safe thing, then."

"The way I do it, it's an acceptable risk."

"Sure."

"It's about not getting greedy," he said. "Every time you make a hundred dollars, you want to keep going."

"Mm."

"But you're always playing against the temptation. That's what's so thrilling. That you can always be tempted."

"To be greedy?"

"Yeah."

"For sure."

≈

Her parents lived a ten-minute drive from campus, but Lara assumed she was spending Christmas getting very high and watching slasher movies with Tess, who also didn't have anywhere to go. Lara's mother explained that it would probably be better if she didn't come to the extended family gathering, but that she could come by later for a "private" Christmas dinner. Lara waited for her mother to text her when the "private" Christmas would be, and then soon enough it was the first of January.

Aaron texted her: *Happy New Year!*

She woke up on Tess's couch, showered, and went home. She removed a pile of clothes from the chair by the window and curled up in it, going through her phone. Frost edged the exterior of her window. Outside, all you could see was a sloped shingle roof with steam curling and billowing out of a chimney pipe.

Winter break was another two weeks.

You're not supposed to text this number except to make an appointment, she texted Aaron. Then she texted her friend Alexis, like she usually did in January, when she would come back from the East Coast.

hey, are you in town for break this yr?

She responded quickly: *yes! i got in ln. want to get coffee or something?*

oh you know I do. white table?

where else

friday?

down. 3 maybe?

Lara had been friends with Alexis in high school when they were both precocious and bullied, and Alexis had come out as a lesbian pretty immediately after leaving. It took Lara another year. When she posted about it on Facebook, Alexis texted *oh my god bitch I fucking knew it* and Lara had been too overwhelmed to respond for a week.

On Friday, Lara got there a little early and Alexis was already there, sitting in the corner with a copy of Franny and Zooey and a pot of tea. She was wearing a pink cable-knit sweater and earrings shaped like inverted triangles. Lara ordered a drip coffee and sat down across from her. She looked up, smiled, and set her book aside.

"Hey, lady," Alexis said.

"Hey yourself."

"You look good."

"Thank you," Lara said. "I like your earrings. Are those pink triangles?"

"Well. Yes."

"I like them. How's the Salinger?" Lara said.

Alexis stuck the book in her bag. "I reread Nine Stories on the plane back," she said. "I feel like I'm regressing."

"Regressing?"

"You know. Whenever I'm in town I feel like a teenager. It's almost as if nothing changed. I mean, I'm sure it's different for you."

"Maybe," Lara said, sipping her coffee.

"This place might still be alive for you."

"Define *alive*."

"Fair."

"Nothing ever changes in Ann Arbor," Lara said.

"Isn't that the truth," Alexis said.

"Are you still working at the archive?"

"Mmhm. It's part of my thesis now, I guess."

"I forgot if you told me about that."

"It's just the same stuff I've been telling you forever, probably. The involvement of lesbians in ACT UP organizing work, economies of care surrounding the AIDS crisis, all that. It's gone from just being literary to, like, actually approximating a historical project."

"Any conclusions yet?"

"Nah. I have some suspicions, but I'm still pretty early on. Are you working on anything interesting? You're still a philosophy major, right?"

"No, I switched into English so I could do a thesis."

"That's exciting. What's your topic?"

"Henry James. Postmodern bullshit. Y'know."

"We don't have to talk about it," Alexis said, twirling a strand of her silky blonde hair. "I don't mean to lead with work."

Lara noticed a man looking at them over the top of his laptop. When she looked at him his eyes returned to his screen.

She could have imagined it. Even if she hadn't, she thought, you can't try to find something behind every sideways look directed at you. You'll go crazy.

She turned back to Alexis, who said, "Everything ok?"

"Yeah," Lara said. "Sorry, I thought I saw someone I knew."

"That will happen," Alexis said. "You know who I ran into the other day?"

"Who?"

"Moira O'Neil. We were in line for the same thing. I didn't know she was in New York."

Lara shifted uncomfortably in her seat, looked down at the table.

"I didn't know that either," she said. "How's she doing?"

"She's ok. She's gotten a lot less, you know, unpredictable. Holding down a job at MacMillan and everything. Do you still talk to her at all?"

"No."

"I don't know what you ever saw in her. She had this doltish boyfriend in tow, some finance guy who was acting super standoffish."

"Sure," Lara said, clenching and unclenching her hand under the table.

"Now that I'm more like, *visibly* queer," Alexis said, "I'm discovering this new thing where guys feel threatened by me in some way."

"I know that feeling," Lara said. "Boyfriend is a precarious position to be in."

"They all seem to think so," Alexis said.

"My friend's boyfriend just proposed to her," Lara said.

"Is that good or bad?"

"Mixed," Lara said. "He asked during finals week. She was kind of mad at him for asking? Last I heard, she told him she'd have an answer when he got back from Minnesota."

"Promising."

"The weird thing is," Lara said, "she's brilliant, and confident, and gorgeous, and throws great parties. She can read Ancient Greek and French, she's probably gonna go to Columbia or Yale or wherever for grad school. He's just like, a middling engineering student."

"Maybe he's great in bed," Alexis said. "Did you ever, like, ask her about this?"

"What would I say?" Lara said. "*Jenna, your boyfriend is too dumb for you?* It's not like I can choose who she likes, it's just a mystery to me, that's all."

"Maybe she needs to hear it," Alexis said.

"Kenny is back from Minnesota tomorrow, actually," Lara said. "I guess I'll know soon."

"Can I meet Jenna?" Alexis said, smiling slightly. "You've intrigued me."

"I can ask."

"Please do," Alexis said. "I'm bored out of my mind here. I need someone new to talk to."

"She's one of my favorite people," Lara said. "I don't want you to think I don't like her. She's always been there for me."

"You can't ask for more than that," Alexis said, with a smile Lara couldn't guess the meaning of. They changed the subject.

≈

When Lara reached Jenna's doorstep a few days later she heard her arguing with someone inside. She knocked, then just let herself in.

Jenna was standing in the middle of the room holding a wine glass and talking on the phone with someone. She looked surprised when she saw Lara, who mouthed, *Ready to go?* at her. Jenna nodded and ducked into her bedroom, where she hung up and reemerged wearing a blue dress and a big parka.

"My mom," Jenna said apologetically.

"No worries," Lara said.

"Yeah, you know." Lara thought Jenna looked a little worried as she closed and locked the door to her apartment.

"I'm looking forward to meeting your friend," Jenna said once they were downstairs.

"Yeah, she is too."

"She's like, queer studies–oriented, right?"

"Yeah."

"Cool. I'll try not to embarrass myself."

Jenna seemed preoccupied and kept staring off into the distance when Lara tried to talk to her. When they got to the bar, Alexis was already there, in a booth by a window. She was drinking a gin and tonic and reading *The Remains of the Day*. She waved to Lara.

Lara sat down next to Alexis and introduced the two of them. Jenna formally shook her hand, which Alexis seemed a little affronted by. Lara took in the contrast between them: Alexis was wearing an asymmetrical leather jacket and those pink triangle earrings that Lara had secretly decided were tacky. She was a few inches taller than Jenna, who looked comparatively tame in her practical winter coat and boots.

"I've heard about you," Alexis said.

"Oh god, Lara, what have you told her."

"Only good things."

"I'll choose to be reassured," Jenna said.

"Lara told me you're *brilliant*."

"That's not quite the word I would use," Jenna said.

They went through the inevitable sparring stage — comparing reference points, talking about past work, talking about ambitions. None of them had really *done* anything yet, so most of the conversation was inevitably about interests, directions, speculations, "ideas."

Lara checked her phone. She texted Tess back about something relating to the lease they were signing together next year. When she looked up, Jenna was leaning on the table with one elbow. She was looking at the taller other woman with wide eyes, as if she was taking notes with her other hand. Alexis noticed this, leaned back in the booth and narrowed her eyes slightly, periodically looking away to make some point or another before training her gaze back on Jenna. Jenna, who either didn't pick up on the fact that Lara's friend was eye-fucking her or liked it, widened her eyes and listened to Alexis's easy, low voice.

This is too much, Lara thought. *Way too much*. She went to the bathroom, and by the time she got back, Kenny had arrived, playing the usual role he had in bringing the conversation down to a tepid, coed level.

"Oh, hi, Lara," he said. "Long time no see."

"We were just talking about how weird Ken's parents are," Jenna said.

"Yeah, they're old hippies," Kenny said. "They were a little disappointed at how boring I turned out."

Lara looked at Alexis, who had a blank, patient expression on her face.

"How's the thesis going, Lara?" he said. "Still working on, what's his name, James something — "

"Henry James," Lara said.

"The Master," Alexis said dryly.

"Oh, let's not talk about *work*," Jenna said.

"We don't have to," Lara said with relief.

"Yeah, we already had, like, *shoptalk* hour before Ken showed up," Jenna said, a little drunk already.

It was the first time Lara had seen Jenna and Kenny together since the conversation outside the library. There was supposed to be a verdict by now, and Lara was looking for some change in Jenna's demeanor, some indication of *temporariness* that was missing before, a signal of a definite change. What hadn't changed was how Kenny kept sneaking glances at her. Lara didn't feel like reciprocating anymore. She felt frustratingly marginal to this entire situation.

She reached out her leg experimentally and nudged Kenny's foot. He started and looked up at Lara, who made a point of not looking at him. When she did it a second time he didn't react, and she let her foot linger there for a beat before withdrawing it and then returning it to his leg a little higher, above his ankle. Watching him out of the corner of her eye, she tucked her hair behind her ear and laughed at something Alexis said.

With the top of her foot she caressed the back of Kenny's calf through his khakis. She looked over at him briefly and noticed that his face had assumed a drawn-in, concentrated look.

"I'll be right back," Lara said. She got up and headed for the bathroom.

"Lara," said Kenny's voice from behind her.

She turned. He approached her with a concerned look.

"Lara, what are you doing?"

She didn't know what to say.

"If this is some kind of power play or something, I — I just don't know what to say. Jen and I are already in a rough spot right now, and you're my *friend*. I don't know what you — "

He was standing really close to her now, close enough to see the lines forming on his forehead as he talked to her. She could feel sweat beading on her back under her dress. She felt like at any moment gravity was going to pull her through the floor. She heard herself apologize in vague, general terms, heard him say "it's all right" with the same unnerved expression on his face, watched him head back to the table. On her way back from the bathroom, Lara ordered a shot and a beer.

Lara and Kenny were both nearly silent for the remainder of the night, but Alexis and Jenna didn't seem to notice. Lara studiously avoided looking at Kenny, but a few times he looked at her, and it was like his eyes were burning a hole through her head. She got more drunk.

It was dark and snowing when they got outside. They did the polite get-home-safe-nice-to-meet-you-see-you-sometime thing and then Jenna and Kenny walked in the opposite direction from Lara and Alexis.

"God, what dull people," Alexis said when they were out of earshot. "Kenny especially."

"She loves him," Lara said, slurring her words a bit. "She's probably gonna marry him."

"Wasn't she like, going to say no to his proposal?"

"Maybe. I dunno. I think they're doing great. They're great for each other," Lara said, slipping a little on a patch of black ice hidden under snow.

Alexis laughed. "You're *drunk*, Lara lady. Maybe she loves him, but they're too young. I'm opposed to him on principle."

"I'm opposed too," Lara said in a smear of syllables.

"Good."

"Where are we walking?" Lara said.

They had just come up to the disused train tracks that marked the border of downtown. Alexis stopped and looked Lara in the eyes. Her breath made a little cloud in front of her face.

"Lara," she said, drunkenly cheerful, "do you want to come back to mine? My parents are gone for the weekend."

"Yeah, I do," Lara said unhesitatingly.

"Okay, then, we're walking this way."

They crossed the train tracks. Beyond them, the streetlights were unevenly spaced, making odd shadows on the snowdrifts. Every so often a car drove by, muffled by the wet snow.

Alexis eventually led Lara up to one of those beautiful Arts and Crafts houses on the west side, with a little plaque from the historical society at the back of the tall, wide porch next to the door. As Alexis fumbled with her keys Lara turned around, imagining what it would be like for this to be your window on the world.

When they were inside Alexis brushed snow off Lara's jacket in the dark entryway. They wordlessly took off their coats. Underneath her jacket, Lara was wearing a tight purple ribbed sweater that showed off her figure. Alexis reached out to brush some snow off Lara's shoulder in a gesture that became an acquisitive, indulgent stroke down to Lara's waist. They locked eyes and Alexis, smiling like she knew a secret, pressed Lara against the front door and kissed her briefly, then pulled away.

"Upstairs," she said.

The stairs creaked. Lara couldn't see very much in the dark rooms. She felt like a teenager again, sneaking around in someone else's house.

Alexis's room was huge and had a double bed inset into a big bay window, through which Lara could see that it was only snowing harder now. In between were bookshelves and bean bag chairs, an open violin case, posters and prints on the walls. There was a shelf full of childhood things — oil pastels, asymmetrical handmade ceramics, two dolls with stringy yellow hair. When she flicked the light switch, two red Chinese lanterns hanging from the center of the ceiling lit up.

"My childhood bedroom," Alexis said, with only some irony. She sat down on the edge of her bed, and Lara sat next to her. Alexis stroked Lara's thigh with her hand.

"It's, like, a preservationist project of my mother's," Alexis went on. "It's important to her that I be reminded that I was twelve once."

Lara rested her head on Alexis's shoulder. Alexis turned and kissed her again, and then nudged her down on her back. She straddled Lara's hips and grasped the back of her head while sticking her tongue in Lara's mouth. Lara liked it but wasn't sure where to put her hands, eventually settling for Alexis's waist. She just left them there, and lay there, and didn't do anything until Alexis stopped, pulled away from her, and looked down, her silky hair forming a curtain around their faces.

"Is something wrong?" Alexis said in a soft voice, a voice that was the opposite of the nasal growl she normally used.

Lara didn't say anything, but her facial expression must have conveyed something, because after a beat Alexis said, "That's fine. I'm too tired anyway."

They both lay down next to each other, looking up at the snow collecting at the top of the bay window the head of the bed was set into.

Alexis said, "I'm so sorry if I did anything that, you know — "

Her voice was so soft, so gentle, so genuinely concerned and unguarded.

"Don't worry about it," Lara said.

Her bed was soft and deep. Lara felt like she was being swallowed. She lay her ankle over Alexis's, who in response curled her whole body up against Lara's — a familiar, affectionate gesture.

"Is this ok?" Alexis said.

"Yeah," Lara said.

There was another long silence. Lara looked up at the churning, purple sky.

"It doesn't snow like this in New York," Alexis said.

"Really?"

"Maybe once or twice a year," Alexis yawned. "Most of last winter, it was just gross and rainy."

"Do you miss the winter?"

"Yeah," she said into Lara's shoulder.

They both fell asleep after that.

≈

"I felt bad for messing with her boyfriend," Lara said to Aaron. "I think I read too much into it."

She was sitting at his dining room table like always. He had arms folded over his chest, listening intently, smiling a little. She was holding, in her arms, a bouquet of white roses he had given her when he opened the door.

"My friend, Tess, she says I have anger issues, and I used to disagree — you know, I'm kind of a passive person. But what I realized is, Tess is right, I *am* an angry person, but I don't go about it the normal way. Instead of blowing up at people, I just get progressively meaner to them if they do something I don't like, or *are* something I don't like. Like, you know, he's my friend's fiancé, and he has this creepy staring thing like I told you. So I, like, get condescending, harass him a little. But I also wonder if I was just imagining the staring. And, you know, the thing with him is that he wants *me* to be the one to make an advance. He doesn't want to *own* it, he wants *just* enough plausible deniability, and *anyway*, I went home with Alexis, the lesbian — "

He was loving this. Grinning. Lara was certain he felt like he was getting the realistic trans girlfriend experience. She was also certain that the flowers meant that at some point, he expected to finally go from the kitchen table to the bedroom, and it somehow seemed so anticlimactic.

She was wrong about that, but he did kiss her on the way out. Lara graciously reciprocated, let him feel her up a bit, waited for him to take it in another direction, but he pulled away and smiled that stupid, fatherly smile.

"See you, Katie," he said.

"See you," Lara said, six hundred dollars richer. What a weirdo. That was gonna be the last time. She would find some other way to make money, she wasn't cut out for this.

After she got off the bus, she walked over to Jenna's apartment and buzzed the door.

"Here," Lara said, handing her the white roses.

"Wait, did he tell you already?" Jenna said.

"What?"

She grinned, turned around, and didn't say anything. Lara sat down on her couch while she put the roses in a vase and set them on the countertop. That done, Jenna came back and sat next to Lara, drew her knees to her chest.

"I said yes," she said.

Lara's eyes widened.

"Congratulations," she managed, about five seconds too late.

They hugged, but Jenna had clearly deflated a little, and Lara was certain she couldn't hide the apprehension she felt.

They recovered from that, and Lara went back to her usual role as someone who listened and nodded. They were going to be fine. Nothing could break Jenna's spirit, probably, and Kenny'd make a lot of money. The sense she had of this as some personal betrayal was totally misplaced. Alexis had been wrong about them. They were conventional, maybe, but not dull.

"Enough about me," Jenna finally said.

Lara blinked.

"What?" she said.

Jenna cocked her head to the side and smiled. She had been caught not listening, but Jenna was clearly so happy it was impossible to bother her with even that. She just wanted to listen to herself talk.

"Lara, Lara. You're my best friend in the world," she said. "You're the second one to know about this. You and my mom. I told her not to tell my dad, I don't even know why. I feel sort of crazy," she said suddenly. "Do you think I'm making the right decision?"

Lara paused. Her eyes slid from Jenna's face to the roses on the countertop, then back to Jenna, whose smile started to crack under the weight of Lara's confused, half-comprehending expression.

"Of course," Lara said, and tried to smile. She was coming to understand how dishonest she had been to her friend, but there was no going back.

"Good," Jenna said fiercely. "Because I am." She stood up, and Lara heard the telltale sound of a pair of wine glasses being lifted out of the dish rack.

"You seem kinda out of it," Jenna said from the kitchen. "Are you, like, alright?"

"Yeah," Lara said. "Sorry. I'm tired. This was a weird semester."

"I totally understand that," Jenna said. "I mean, you saw me that night at the library. I wasn't sure if I was gonna make it."

"But you did," Lara said absentmindedly.

"Yes," Jenna said. Her perfect, unshakable confidence was back to stay. "Yes. You will too."

Means to an End

All summer, my roommate Adelaide's cat kept escaping through the window at night. She usually never got far — into the trees in the courtyard, a couple times scaling the fire escape to the roof. But once she made it all the way down the block to Fresh Pond Road, where my other roommate Nadine found her, clinging to the lowest branch of a street tree, looking down at the sidewalk with wide, terrified eyes. Nadine waved me over from where I was looking underneath cars.

"This is the last time I'm doing this for you, the last *fucking* time," Nadine said in the lilting, singsong voice you would use to talk to a baby, extending her arms up toward the orange animal. "Isn't that *right*, kitty? I'm never doing this again, *no*, not for you and not for your mommy, hmm? If you get out again, it's between you and Addy, hmm?"

The cat meowed mournfully and clutched the branch tighter. People were getting on and off the subway nearby, and men were sitting outside on folding chairs in front of a barbershop. A few people curiously watched Nadine, and one guy paused to take a video with his cell phone. A woman like her, noticeably out of place in one of New York's last real working-class neighborhoods, trying to cajole a somewhat feral cat out of a tree — it *was* funny.

I tried to imagine what the video would look like to someone who didn't know Nadine. She had an innocent aspect to her — she was rather short, had a round face, dark brown hair that she kept in a low-maintenance bob, an unassuming style of dress. It took a while to see the intensity under the surface.

I called Adelaide. While I was waiting for her to pick up, I flipped off the guy taking the video, which might have been overkill, but it did make him keep walking.

"We found her," I said. "She's ok." Nadine had gotten the cat out of the tree and was easing her into the cat carrier.

"Oh my god, thank you so much," Adelaide said. From the swirling murmur of city sounds behind her voice I figured she was outside her office in Manhattan. "I'm so sorry this always seems to happen when I'm not there. I owe you. Where was she?"

"Fresh Pond," I said.

"God," she said. "Fuck. I'm so glad you found her before anything happened."

"You need to keep that window closed," I said.

"Yeah, you're right. Sorry. Um, I have to go. I've been a mess today. I need to, like, not get fired."

The cat was pressing its little face against the plastic mesh of the carrier and making throaty complaining sounds. Nadine held it at a distance from her, grimacing slightly.

"I deserve some kind of award for not biting her head off about this," Nadine said.

"I know what you mean," I said.

"Would you mind taking her back?"

"Not at all."

She handed me the cat carrier and walked off down the street in the opposite direction from our building. I watched her fumble in her purse to get her phone and call somebody, but by then she was out of earshot.

Eight months ago, Adelaide's housing situation fell apart, and she had crashed on our couch for what was supposed to be a month. Something to do with having burned through the good graces of most of her other friends from school — I didn't ask. A month turned into two, and at some point Adelaide started sleeping in Minna's room and paying half of Minna's rent, a situation Nadine quickly grew to resent.

Then, Adelaide found the cat on the subway tracks near Prospect Park late at night. It proceeded to kill four of Nadine's plants, break a dozen different pieces of glassware, scratch up the couch, and escape six times in two months. Nadine asked Adelaide for money to cover the cost of the things that had fallen victim to the cat. Adelaide quickly replaced the plants and the glassware but was reluctant to buy a new couch. Then, Nadine insisted that the cat stay in Minna and Adelaide's bedroom, which Adelaide flat-out refused to do. Both of them used the language of "setting boundaries" and "shared space," and it became a stalemate. Then, Nadine started taking issue with everything Adelaide did — her messiness, her habits, the way she "monopolized" Minna.

"I feel like she's taking me *hostage*," Nadine said to me once after arguing with Adelaide. Whenever Nadine got into an argument with her, or merely felt disrespected, she'd want to talk to me. I would affirm her feelings and otherwise stay out of it.

I didn't share Nadine's dislike of her, but Adelaide knew I was Nadine's confidante, so it was natural that she was a little cagey around me. I wasn't sure if Adelaide fully understood the extent of Nadine's irritation. If she did, it didn't bother her. The few times I talked with her directly about it, she had a calm, insouciant equanimity about the whole situation.

"I think we just have different ideas about what an apartment should be like," Adelaide told me once. "That's basically it, right? Nadine doesn't want to have to adjust the way she lives."

"And neither do you," I said.

"Exactly!" Adelaide said, smiling. "I'm conceding to *some* of her ridiculous demands and not others. It's compromise."

The apartment was empty when I got back. The kitchen was strewn with dishes and empties. I let the cat out on the floor and it immediately sprinted through the open door to

Minna and Adelaide's bedroom. I refilled my water bottle and went out back to light up. I blew a cloud of smoke, watched it slowly dissipate. Across the courtyard someone opened a window, and a slow, swaying accordion tune piped faintly out. Behind me, I heard the sounds of Minna making a late breakfast.

The backyard was where I did most of my thinking. It was a quiet, private space overgrown with ivy and burdock, surrounded by other five-story brick buildings. Clotheslines crossed between buildings. During the summer, Adelaide would bring the cat outside with her while she answered emails and chain-smoked. The cat would jump over the fence and roam around in the enclosed courtyard, eventually coming back to Adelaide to get scratched behind the ears, or, a couple times, to display a dead rat or pigeon to her. Adelaide never talked baby talk to the cat, the way Nadine and Minna and I all did constantly.

Minna opened the back door and sat down next to me on the top step, holding a plate of scrambled eggs with mushrooms and stringy spinach.

"Hey Leo," she said. "I saw the texts about the cat when I woke up, but she's back at her usual place."

"You guys gotta close that window," I said.

"We opened it from the top this time," she said. "There was, like, two inches of space on the top of the window, and she still got out. Maybe we need to get the screen replaced. Can I hit that, by the way?"

I handed her the little glass piece and my lighter. She set the plate down and closed her big, green eyes while maneuvering the flame over the small clump of weed in the bottom of the bowl. Minna's room was a closet, and with the addition of Adelaide's belongings was now full to the brim with clothes, records, books, posters, makeup, and knickknacks, and Nadine didn't let them put the litter box in the living room, so that was in there too. I couldn't blame them for wanting to keep the window open in the middle of August.

Adelaide complained often about the crampedness of the room, but I never heard Minna mention it. I wondered often if Nadine was in love with Minna. At minimum they used to be good friends, and there was something about Adelaide — tall, slender Adelaide, who had cascading curly hair the color of wheat and long, strong hands — that got under Nadine's skin. Minna seemed to see her relationship with Adelaide as worth whatever trouble it was causing Nadine, and this hurt Nadine a lot more than anything Adelaide could do.

"What do you have going on today?" Minna asked, handing the piece back and starting on her eggs.

"Nothing," I said. I checked my phone, scrolled through inane notifications from social media.

Nadine had texted me: *went to that coffee place on forest kinda want to avoid the apartment today "lol"*

could/should I come by? I texted back.

"I sorta figured, you know, given the weed," Minna said. "No judgment, though. What's the damage with Nadine, by the way?"

"The usual damage, I think," I said.

Nadine replied: *ya come through, randomly ran into my friend who I think you'd like*

"I feel like I haven't had time to think all week," Minna said, looking up at the sky.

A few seconds later, Nadine added: *I promise I'm not as mad as I sounded earlier*

"I know what you mean," I said.

She smiled one of her totally disarming smiles. "When will it end," she said. "I should probably, like, figure out the window."

"Yeah, I'm gonna go on a walk, I think," I said.

"See ya."

The coffee shop Nadine had gone to was designed from the same template as the one I worked at in Williamsburg, all white tile and imposing, well-cared-for tropical plants next to the big windows. Nadine was sitting at a table on the patio with someone I didn't recognize, a woman about our age wearing a big t-shirt dress and chunky plastic sunglasses. I sat down in the available third chair.

"Hi Leonora," Nadine said, not really looking at me. "Have you two met?"

Her companion was lighting a cigarette. She looked up at me disinterestedly and we both shook our heads politely at each other.

This was way back before I knew any other trans women. I knew that New York was full of them, but somehow they had all avoided me up until this point. When she spoke I realized, belatedly, that I had finally found one.

"I'm Violet," she said.

"I'm Leonora," I said.

"That's a beautiful name," Violet said.

"Thank you."

"Do you know the writer Leonora Carrington?"

"No," I said.

"Oh, well, never mind. I was just thinking that it would be cool to meet someone who named herself after Leonora Carrington."

"Sorry," I said.

I probably didn't think of anything better because I was surprised that she acknowledged that I'm trans (people usually ignored it) in a way that really foregrounded something else — namely, that I wasn't as sophisticated as her. Another person whose life was different enough from mine that our universes of small talk were totally incompatible. The longer it had been since college, the more my life was filling up with these people.

"Violet is one of my good exes," Nadine said.

"I don't know if I'm *good*," Violet said. There was a hint of a laugh in her voice.

"You're *better*," Nadine said.

"Low bar," Violet said.

This sounds so lame, but at that point I wanted to get up and leave. Violet, I was gleaning, was miles ahead of me. I felt ashamed to even be sitting at the table with her. I had only been on estrogen for a few months, but I had no idea that *this* was what I could have been aiming for. Watching her flirt with Nadine made me feel like I had been crazily undervaluing the potential my future life had. Like, fuck, at minimum I needed a haircut and some new clothes —

"Okay, anyway, that was a lot about me," Nadine said, referencing some earlier thread in the conversation. "How's work?"

Violet sighed theatrically. "Good. Bad. The same. I'm, like, having the same fight with my manager I was having in December, but I think there's a limit to how far it can go this time."

"Where do you work?" I said.

She named an art gallery in Lower Manhattan that I had heard of, and I told her that I had heard of it, and she nodded politely.

"It's, you know, *prestige*, but it's mostly normal office work," she said. "I complain about it a lot, but it's, like, fine. It beats serving coffee."

"I know what you mean," I said.

I looked over at Nadine, who was looking up above the awning at the pair of pigeons nesting in the eaves of the building.

"What do you do?" Violet said.

"I'm a writer," I said.

She nodded thoughtfully.

I was literally twitching in my seat at that point, so I abruptly and awkwardly made some dumb excuse to leave. Nadine stood to hug me, and Violet waved from her seat.

"Nice to meet you, Leonora," she said, looking me in the face.

On my way back down the block I could hear Violet talking in that loud, nasal voice about the office politics at that stupid art gallery. I heard her call another woman a "dumb bitch," some coworker or interlocutor, and I heard Nadine laugh, and then I turned the corner.

☙

"I feel like that cat would be happier on the street," Nadine said. "Like, I feel like in our apartment she's always just stressed out and constrained. That's probably why she destroys things. She's trying to tell us — *please, I don't belong here.*"

It was a couple days later and we were walking somewhere together. She was texting rapidly while walking.

"Violet wanted to invite you to a party she's hosting next week, by the way," Nadine said. "Her roommate and her new girlfriend are doing a housewarming, even though they've been in that apartment for six months."

"Sure," I said.

"I think Violet is outgrowing the lesbian poets," Nadine said. "She wants to make new friends."

I turned over the phrase *outgrowing the lesbian poets* in my head. Each word seemed to imply a different facet of Violet's life that further indicated how different she was from me.

"I'll go, yeah," I said.

"She's a good one, Violet," Nadine said. "Sort of the one who got away."

She never said much about her inner life — what she desired or feared or regretted. I imagined that she had a mind that never stopped moving, that she didn't want to interrupt herself by trying to put her feelings into words.

"You two still have chemistry," I offered.

"Something like that," she said, and changed the subject.

※

What do you do?
I'm a writer.
Lately, whenever I wrote anything down, even if just in my diary, I imagined someone smarter than me methodically and mercilessly taking it apart, refuting my every claim, no matter how provisional. I gradually stopped putting anything on paper. I spent a lot of time thinking about how this might change.

At the coffee shop, I would stop thinking about anything. I focused my entire being on the next thing to do. The same few images and phrases turned over in my head until they were worn smooth like pieces of quartz in a rock tumbler. I whistled little snippets of melody from pop songs until they didn't sound like music anymore.

Most of the time I was working with Angelie, a stage actor from Iowa. She spent all her breaks smoking Marlboro Lights on the sidewalk looking at Instagram. If not for the apron she would have looked a lot like the clientele. Her clothes were all expensive-looking, slightly too big on her, and either black, bleach-white, or gray. She had a rotating cast of boyfriends who all loved to visit her at work, looking busy and rich. She seemed lost in a fantasy of her own life. She picked the playlists. We didn't really talk.

On Friday I locked the door, pulled down the grate, and looked down Driggs Avenue at the gathering purple of the sky. I could just make out the beginnings of the bridge, murmuring with traffic.

When I got home, Adelaide and Minna were in the back yard.

"Hey," Minna said. "Haven't seen much of you these past few days."

"The girl works six days a week," Adelaide said, without looking up from her phone.

"So true," I said.

I sat on the upturned milk crate after yanking it out from one of the ganglier burdocks.

The sky was a gentle pale blue gradient above the unbroken rows of buildings. The world felt still and open.

"You doing anything tonight, Leo?" Adelaide said.

"Yeah," I said. I had forgotten about the party until that moment. I texted Nadine, who sent me the address and told me that it had already started.

"Oh, are you going to that housewarming party at Katie's?" Minna said.

"Yeah."

"Vi Rodriguez lives there too, right?" Adelaide said. "Did you know she and Nadine used to date?"

"I did know that," I said.

"Right," Minna said. "I remember that. Even at the time I thought it was weird."

"Yeah, it's like Morticia Addams dating the Grinch," Adelaide said.

We all had a good laugh at that.

"If you ever get a chance to talk to Vi about Nadine, take it," Minna said. "She has some crazy stories."

"Like what?"

Minna and Adelaide exchanged a glance, the meaning of which I couldn't determine at all.

"I don't know if I'm at liberty to say," Adelaide said. She twisted a strand of her hair around her index finger.

"Let's just say that her relationship with Nadine was what made her decide to, like, exclusively date other trans people," Minna said.

"Now none of us have a chance with Morticia Addams," Adelaide said.

"Leo still has a chance," Minna said playfully.

I was tempted to pry, but this felt like dangerous territory, and I had to leave anyway.

The subway was delayed, and by the time I got there, it was dark. I wasn't meeting many people in those days, and whenever I ended up in a stranger's apartment, I noticed everything. There was a grimy window in the stairwell that had a view of the streetlights and winding paths of Maria Hernandez Park, a gigantic playing card laid flat. When I knocked on the door a pair of women answered, one significantly taller than the other with her arm around the other's waist. They introduced themselves as Katie and Sophie, and then Sophie ran off.

"What was your name again?" Katie said. She had the same nasal tenor with a little bit of a rasp under the lowest notes that Violet had. It was like her voice was on stilts.

"Leonora."

"That's a beautiful name."

She offered me a drink and I accepted a cup of white wine, then I went to the bathroom and looked at my phone for a few minutes while drinking it. When I finished, I filled the cup with water and drank that in two big gulps, then I opened the door and re-entered the party.

Katie and Violet's apartment was a larger and better-decorated version of the one I lived in. There was a big bookshelf and some tasteful, expensive-looking furniture. I recognized a few of Nadine's grad school cohort, professional people having difficulty relaxing, and a few of whom I gathered were the "lesbian poets," who were dressed flamboyantly and mostly talked to each other.

I didn't know anyone here, really. Nadine was in the corner, but she was deep in conversation with two women from her program and looked unapproachable at the moment. No one noticed me as I went to the kitchen to get another drink. As I was pouring gin into my wine glass, someone tapped me on the shoulder. It was Violet.

"Hiya," she said, and hugged me.

When she let go of me I got a good look at her. She was wearing a big, shoulderless black dress and had a silver chain dangling down below her Adam's apple. She had the middle finger of her left hand poised over her bottom lip.

"Let me introduce you," she said. I noticed a small circle of trans women in the corner of the kitchen. Violet rejoined them and got their attention.

"Katie, Veronica, Sarah, Helen, this is Leonora," Violet said, pointing to each of the girls in turn. They all nodded politely.

"So, you're the fourth tenant of the lesbian love triangle apartment," Veronica said to me.

"That's me."

Veronica was wearing a dress that hugged her bony frame with long, bell-like sleeves. She looked like a witch, a conjurer. It occurred to me that they all knew something I didn't, which is that you only have one body and it's useless to hide it when you're among friends.

Lost in thought, I almost didn't notice when everyone in this little circle started for the other side of the kitchen, toward a spiral staircase that led up into a circular hole in the ceiling. I poured more gin into my cup and followed them. Veronica wedged open a little trap door at the top and a warm breeze of summer air flowed down over us.

Violet and I were the last ones out on the roof, and we hung back while the rest of them walked to the side of the roof that faced the glittering, apparitional masses of Manhattan.

She lit a cigarette.

"How was your week?" she said, as if she checked in like this all the time, just a continuation of a long acquaintance.

"It was okay. I was working a lot."

"Me too," she said.

"Has it gotten better than last time?"

"Yes," she said. "A lot better."

"I'm glad to hear that."

"Hey, I have a weird question for you," she said. "Is it true that you're nineteen years old?"

"Twenty," I said.

"Got it," she said. "Nadine said that you're, like, some kind of prodigy. She tends to exaggerate when she likes someone. You should take it as a compliment."

"I had to drop out of school," I said.

"I heard," she said simply. "I'm sorry."

"It's okay," I said. "I'm gonna go back once I can figure out how to pay for it."

She nodded. "How'd you end up living with Nadine?"

"She TA'd a poetry class I was in at NYU," I said. "And, you know, we knew each other. I sort of, um, found out suddenly that I had to leave, you know, leave the dorms at the end of the term, and she found me and just point-blank told me that Cody was moving out and that I could live with her if I wanted to."

"Gotcha," Violet said. "Moving in with your teacher is intense."

"I mean, you know, I was just thinking practically," I said, talking faster and faster, clenching my hands inside the pockets of my dress. "You know that apartment is really crazy cheap. The only other option I could have afforded was, like, living with my sister in her place in Bensonhurst that she shares with her fiancé."

"Oh, naturally," Violet said. "I lived in South Brooklyn for a year while I was in graduate school and it was terrible."

"I didn't want to be isolated," I finished.

"Understandable," she said. "You're around a lot of, like, older people now."

"I mean, everyone is like, twenty-four, twenty-six," I said, waving my hand. "It's not a huge difference."

She nodded.

"I'm kind of curious how you're dealing with the cold war between Nadine and Adelaide," she said. "I'm like, extremely tangential to the whole thing."

For the first time, I looked her square in the face. It was a good face, I decided. Hollowed-out cheeks, residues of stubble dotting her chin and neck. Only her posture indicated that she was sure of anything. Her eyes were clear and steady on me. This was someone who was on my side, I realized.

"It's exhausting," I said.

"Yeah," she said. "You know, between the two of us — when someone told me that the person moving in when Cody left was a trans girl, my first thought was, like, *oh, poor thing*."

"That's me," I said. "I'm the poor thing."

I laughed but it came out sounding sort of bitter. Behind her, Sarah and Veronica were kissing gently and steadily, their bodies indistinct in the half-light.

"As a retired poor thing," she said, "I think Nadine has sort of a *thing* with trans girls."

"Like she's a chaser?"

Violet winced. "No, not a chaser. But I think she has a way of finding trans girls who are newly out, you know?"

I didn't know. "Yeah," I said.

"Nadine has this thing where she's convinced that she's like, a lone wolf, she's very independent, she's had this hard life, and she's figured it all out now. But she's actually very needy. She needs a lot more than she lets on, she needs maybe more than she realizes she needs."

"Oh," I said.

"I mean, don't get me wrong, Adelaide is genuinely a piece of work. You couldn't pay me to live with her. But the thing with Minna feels like it was, like, designed to make Nadine into the most vindictive version of herself. She's sort of decided that she's in the right, and that means she's probably decided that you're on her side, and she won't take the necessary precautions to make sure you're not caught in it."

I looked up at her, and she was looking back at me, with a facial expression that was sort of hesitant, drawn into herself, and I realized that I probably looked the exact same way. Always tentative, unsure.

A feeling of perfect confidence suddenly flowed through me, like the warm breeze that was nudging strands of hair around the sides of her face. I leaned in and kissed her tentatively on the corner of her mouth. She kissed me back, cautiously and then more insistently.

"Okay, okay, okay," she said, laughing. "I need to find out a few more things about you first. Do you wanna go downstairs?"

≈

She was making me a drink in the kitchen, something that required more than two bottles from the countertop. The party started to move up to the roof. I checked my phone and saw that Nadine had texted me something long.

I skimmed over it. *Hey! left early, good to see you at this tonight ... Lease ends September 1 ... adelaide and min are technically breaking occupancy law ... lmk if you have any leads for roommates ...*

"Hi," she said, handing me a red plastic cup.

She was standing close to me, smiling closemouthed, with her head turned to the side in an open question. I put my hand on her waist.

She kissed me, softly at first and then more insistently. Her hands found my waist. I murmured a little bit into her mouth and she kissed me harder, then pulled back.

"Wanna go back to my room?" she whispered.

"In a minute," I said.

We drank our drinks and found a common topic in a writer we both knew, but every word we said after that was a veiled flirtation. It was delaying the inevitable. At some point she just started walking across the room midsentence, and I followed her.

The only decor in her room was, I swear to god, three huge canvases painted the same shade of bright green hung on the wall. Everything else was on the floor. The mattress, a few candles in old wine bottles, a small stack of paperback books, all arranged around the focal point of the window.

I sat on the mattress while she switched on a lamp in the corner.

"How old are you?" I asked.

"Twenty-six," she said. "Does that bother you?"

"No," I said. "I was just curious."

When she sat down on the bed we started making out sloppily, like teenagers in a car. She pulled my dress off over my head and I tugged at hers until she undid the clasp at the back that made it fall off her shoulders. She pushed me down onto my back.

I extended my arms above my head and looked up at her.

"What do you like?" she murmured.

I had no idea. So I said the first thing that came to mind:

"Can you ... hurt me?"

She nodded, which made her hair flop in a curtain around her face.

"Okay," she breathed.

She ran her hands up my thighs, and then when she reached my hips she sank her thumbs into some hollow space in my pelvis. It was so immediate, and so unexpected, that it felt like an electric shock to my brain. I heard myself whimper and arched my back. She dug deeper.

"Harder," I said. It was already excruciating, but I wanted her to test my limits. When I said that, really more moaned it, she abruptly let go of my hips and straddled me. She leaned over and covered my mouth with one hand.

"There's still a party going on," she said with a laugh in her voice. She was holding me down, but just barely. I could have shoved her off with a subliminal nudge.

She kept her hand over my mouth while she twisted my little left breast with three fingers. I made these pathetic whimpering sounds into her palm. I thought I sounded like a poor imitation of girls in porn, and I wanted her to push me to a point where that didn't matter to me anymore.

"*Harder*." I whispered it this time.

Red and green sparks flew in front of my eyes. I grabbed her arm and squeaked.

She let go of me and kissed my mouth hard. With her other hand she was reaching into my underwear and her fingers found my asshole. She put her face very close to mine.

"Is this okay?" she said.

I nodded.

She nudged me onto my hands and knees and pressed down on the small of my back. I felt her reach over me to one side of the bed and get a little bottle of lube.

That gave me some time to come back into my body, there with my face sideways on her bed. I read the spines of her books stacked next to the bed. Some of them were in German, and there was that one novel from the trans press that folded years ago. I wondered if it was worth reading. She stuck one finger in me, then two, and I pressed my face into the mattress. It felt good in a way that wasn't obvious at first, but when I settled into it I felt lucky, so lucky, I almost didn't believe what I was feeling, and then it was over.

When we had cleaned ourselves off and were laying next to each other, I didn't think to tell her that it was my first time as a woman. It didn't feel like I had made a beginning at having sex, it felt like I had wandered into the middle of a game with established rules that I had successfully picked up fast enough. No need to belabor the point.

We went back to gossiping about Nadine, the only topic we had in common, and devised improbable solutions for her life, laughing to each other. She held me until we both fell asleep.

※

On the train platform the next day I fretted about the text I wanted to send her. I had woken up at 7 a.m. totally alert, and I had to be at work in a couple hours. I left her still curled up in the fetal position, facing away from me.

Hey woke up a little early and didn't want to wake you up so I left. Are you free soon?

Woke up early and didn't want to wake you. When can I see you again?

Last night was so lovely, when are you free?

I kept reducing the message I wanted to send until I arrived at: *left early, can I see you again?*

It was totally insufficient but somehow more vulnerable than I wanted. As the time since I had sent the text piled up, into a day and then another, I felt worse and worse about it.

Eventually I asked Nadine:

"Nadine," I started. We were in the grocery store. "What's Violet's deal?"

"She thinks she's smarter than everyone else, and it's because she kinda is," Nadine said without pausing to consider the question. "But at the same time, she's too self-conscious to really make anything happen. That's why she still has that awful job, those boring friends. She's never really failed at anything before, so she doesn't try to do anything hard."

We were standing in the produce section of the grocery store. She said all of this while examining a big bulb of fennel.

"I know you hooked up with her," Nadine said. "She told me. It doesn't bother me."

"Oh."

"How was it?" Nadine said. She put the fennel in her basket and reached for a bunch of rosemary at the top of the shelf.

"It was, uh, good," I said. "Really good."

"Nice," Nadine said in apparent sincerity. "Are you going to see her again?"

"I texted her, but she didn't get back to me."

"Hmm," Nadine said. "Yeah, she'll do that. You should text her again."

"Okay."

"How do you feel about it?" Nadine said.

"Good," I said.

The truth was that I was thinking about Violet constantly. I wanted her to fuck me like that every day. At night, after I turned the lights off, I would writhe under the covers and leave handprint-shaped marks on my breasts from grabbing their sensitive new flesh, trying to push past pain into pleasure the way she had done to me. I put my face into a pillow and pressed my abdomen into the mattress, unsure if I was even turned on, frustrated at my own lack of response.

My feelings about her were blooming into a huge, unrealistic fantasy that made everything else look flat and dull and stupid. The passive-aggressive games of avoidance and feigned obliviousness that my roommates played became exasperating, and I was aware that I was wasting my time at my dumb job. The few friends from school who visited me at work became particularly grating. When I dropped out of school, my friends came up with half-baked solutions or would offer money, accommodations, help of all kinds that I didn't really need and couldn't imagine asking from anyone. Now they just came in for the novelty of knowing a barista's name somewhere. Some of them tipped poorly and some of them tipped 100 percent or more, which were both depressing in different ways.

I was stewing in all this at work when Katie and Veronica came in. Their conversation trailed off as they walked up to the counter and squinted at the menu above my head.

"Oh hey," Katie said. "Did I meet you the other night?"

"Yes," I said.

"Your name is Nora, right?"

"Leonora," I said.

"I was close," Katie said, still scrutinizing the menu. "Do you like Nora as a nickname?"

"I go by Leo sometimes," I said. "I could see it."

"Leo's a good name," Katie said. She looked down at me and smiled. "Can I call you Nora?"

"Yes," I said.

"It's good to see you," Veronica said. "Violet had some nice things to say about you. You should come around more."

"I texted Violet the other day," I said. "She never got back to me."

"She's a terrible texter," Veronica said. "You should just double-text."

They both ordered lattes, and even though I assumed they were fine on money I didn't charge either of them. When I handed Katie her drink she winked at me. They sat in the corner booth by the big plant and talked to each other for the rest of my shift, leaning over the table so their faces were almost touching at points. I tried not to look at them too much.

≈

I went home and showered and smoked a bowl and sat on the couch, considering what I should text Violet.

Hey, I'd like to meet up and talk a bit. The other night took me by surprise, but...

I didn't overthink it this time. I just sent the first thing I typed. Violet texted back immediately, which hit me with a rush of adrenaline.

Yeah I can talk, you free tonight? She named a bar in Bushwick.

At some point, Adelaide and Minna came into the kitchen and started making tea. Whenever they were together in the same room they talked to each other constantly, about the tea, about their friends, about work, about their inane preferences for this thing over that thing. Adelaide had her arm around Minna's waist, both of them facing the counter. Just then, Nadine unlocked the front door and walked in with groceries in two big paper bags. I waved to her but she didn't seem to notice me. Her eyebrows were drawn in, and there was a deliberate, careful way that she took her shoes off and set the bags of groceries down.

"Can one of you do the dishes?" Nadine said.

They pretended not to hear her and went on talking. Minna snuck a nervous glance over her shoulder at where Nadine was standing in the doorway to the kitchen.

"I don't think that's too much to ask," Nadine said. "I do them every day."

"All right," Adelaide said, turning around and facing her. "You're gonna evict us and then we have to clean up after you?"

Minna looked like she wanted to say something but didn't.

"This is *your* mess," Nadine said, gesturing around her at the kitchen. "And I am not 'evicting' you. You're breaking the law, so don't put that on me. Every day I — "

Adelaide interrupted her. "I know for a fact that you used that cast iron yesterday. I was in here when you — "

"Can you please just do it!" Nadine yelled.

"Come on, guys," Minna started to say, but then Nadine and Adelaide started talking loudly at each other, over top of each other.

I wanted to leave but I would have had to walk in front of all of them on my way to my bedroom, so I just sat there.

"You've created an inhospitable environment for me," Nadine finally said. Adelaide trailed off of whatever she was saying and just stood there.

"And?" Adelaide said. "You're weaponizing the law to get us kicked out." Then, Adelaide turned to me. "Leo, isn't it *wrong* to do that?"

"Nadine, back off," I said quietly.

"I'm asking for something simple right now," Nadine said. Her face was red and her eyes were wide and her voice sounded husky. "I let you *walk* all over me," she said pointing a finger at Adelaide, who just stood there smirking.

"I'm not doing your fucking bidding, you psychopath," Adelaide said, and turned around.

Nadine reached for a mason jar on the counter and threw it at Adelaide's head. She missed and it shattered on the cabinet and sent shards flying away in all directions. Adelaide ducked away and Minna let out a scream that was more like a squeak.

"What the FUCK, Nadine!!!" Minna shouted.

I walked over to Nadine, who looked like she had immediately, finally, regretted everything that had led to this point. Her arms were hanging limp by her sides.

"I think we should go for a walk, Nadine," I said, reaching out to touch her arm.

She shoved me away and stormed out herself, leaving those two paper bags on the floor.

None of us talked much. I helped Adelaide sweep the broken glass off the floor. Minna sat on the couch and stared at her knees. When we were done, Adelaide held her as she shook and cried.

I couldn't find Nadine at any of her usual places, and she didn't return a phone call. I didn't know what I would say if I saw her, so I guessed it was all just as well.

~

I called my sister.

"Wait, what the hell? What have you been doing?" she said. "Are you still in New York? You should have a degree by now."

"Ask mom," I said.

"She and I aren't talking right now," she said.

"Oh, you too?" I said sarcastically.

She sighed. "Look, you can go ahead and act like the victim, but it's not like you didn't antagonize her for years. I had to put up with a lot more than you did, for years, yeah? And don't act like it's different because you're trans."

"No, I'm not going to take that," I said, my voice raising into a yell. "She told me she'd rather see me dead. She said that."

"You know what kind of shit she's said to me?" she yelled back, so loud the phone audio started to distort. "I didn't throw a fucking *fit* and drop out of school, Leo."

"She didn't give me a choice," I said. My voice cracked a little on the last word.

"You had a fucking choice," she shouted even louder, if that was possible. "If I had a choice, so did you. Don't act like some fucking *martyr*, I dealt with her because I *had* to. I hope making your little *point* to her was worth it."

"You're a fucking hypocrite," I said.

"And you're a child," she said and hung up.

≈

I was super early to meet up with Violet. I sat on a block of concrete in the street next to a bunch of chairs and tables the bar had set outside, and I tried to distract myself with my phone. Looking at posts on the internet, you can almost feel normal, like you're a member of some chorus, no matter what's going on with you.

Violet was standing in front of me before I noticed her. I was a little startled. She was wearing all black and towed a tall, skinny bike with one hand.

"Hi," I said, stuffing my phone in my purse.

"Hi," Violet said. "It looks crowded in there, wanna just walk?"

Neither of us talked for about a block and a half. The silence started to get unbearable. We turned onto Irving Avenue and passed under the glowing awnings of storefronts.

"So," she finally said. "What's up?"

The way she said it made me think twice about what to say. She sounded curt, formal, like someone getting down to business.

"Um," I started, hoping to form a response midair and failing.

"How's Nadine?" Violet said.

"She's ok, I think."

"Mm."

This was entirely wrong. I wanted to start over.

"Given the circumstances, you know."

"Yeah. I told her she should just move in with me when Zoe moves to Chicago."

"She really doesn't want to leave that apartment," I said.

"Mm."

I couldn't decide whether or not to tell her about what happened a few hours beforehand. If I did, the conversation would be just about that, and I so badly wanted Violet to belong to an entirely different part of my life than all that mess, so I didn't say anything.

The silence was starting to get uncomfortable. She turned onto a little side street and I followed her.

"So, what did you want to talk about?" she said when we were halfway down the block.

"I wanted to say — " I started, then trailed off again.

I looked at her desperately for some sign. There was that same tentative expression, but now it was like a blank wall. She avoided eye contact.

The silence stretched out. We both kept walking.

"I just wanted to see you again," I said.

"For sure," Violet said.

After another long pause, Violet said: "Okay, I'll say this. When you said you wanted to *talk* I sort of assumed the worst, you know?"

"What?"

"You know," she said uneasily. "We were both pretty fucked up that night."

"Yeah," I said. "No, it's not that."

"I was worried I had hurt you," Violet said. "I felt weird about it."

"You didn't hurt me," I said.

"Okay," Violet said. "Good."

We were standing in front of the bar again, after barely fifteen minutes. A few small groups of people were sitting on the benches the bar had installed on the sidewalk, smoking and drinking and talking. She stopped walking.

"Look, I'm sorry," she said. "But I'm not sure what it is you want from me."

"That was the first time I'd had sex with anyone since transitioning," I blurted out.

"That's intense," she said.

I was staring desperately at her face for some sign of what to do next. She was looking at me with an expression of pity, but when she spoke her voice was like iron.

"Okay. Hmm. Where I'm at on this is, if that's what you wanted to talk about, I feel sort of disrespected by the way you've approached me with this."

"Uh-huh."

"I get it, I *represent* something to you. But I wasn't doing you a favor."

"Yeah," I said.

"That makes me feel kind of bad. Like, I'm not a real person to you, I'm an experience. I'm a means to an end." She said all of this like she was already tired of saying it.

"No, it's not like that," I said.

She sighed. "What's it like, then? What do you think I can do for you? Can you *please* just say one definitive thing?"

"I'm sorry," I said.

"You don't have anything to be sorry for," she said.

"I just wanted to see you again," I said. "I hoped we could date, or something."

"Okay," she said. "I mean, look. I'm not upset with you, I'm just — if it's gonna be like this, I can't."

"Yeah," I said.

"We'll see each other again. Just — it can't be like this."
"Okay," I said.
"I'm exhausted," she said. "I'll see you around, Leo."
"See you."

༅

I barely remember getting home after that.

Inside, all the lights were off and Nadine was sitting on the armchair hunched over her laptop, which glowed an angry white, lighting up all the angles of her face.

"Where were you?" she asked.

"With Violet at a bar," I said.

She smiled with her mouth but not her eyes, then sort of wrinkled her face and looked back down at her laptop.

"Our neighbor came by," Nadine said. "Camila, I think her name is. She wanted to know what was going on."

"What did you tell her?"

"I said we had some conflict. I don't know. I'm so fucked up. She was so nice. She thought it was someone's bad boyfriend. I guess I'm the bad boyfriend."

I realized she was very drunk. I sat next to her.

"Leo, you're good," Nadine slurred. "You deserve good things happening to you." She was crying. I leaned over her chair to hug her, and before long, I was crying too.

Her body was so much smaller than mine, so much more fragile, but she clung to me with the force of a cat digging in its claws. She rested her head against my breast and sniffled and mumbled. "I'm sorry I haven't been good to you," she said. "I feel so fucking stupid."

The shoulder of my dress was saturated with tears and snot. She buried her face as deep as it would go in the hollow space of my chest and let out a long, sustained wail.

༅

I woke up to a long text from Violet. It began: *so I feel sorta weird about how I acted last night. I totally understand if you don't want to...*

I turned my phone off and pulled the covers over my head.

Adelaide was sitting on the couch, taking long pulls on her vape, filling the air with strawberry-flavored smoke. Nadine came in, made herself coffee, and left. She had dark circles under her eyes.

It was already afternoon outside, the light was turning soft and forgiving. I realized that I was staring at the big stack of dishes in the sink, untouched since yesterday.

I did the dishes. It took fifteen minutes.

While I did them I thought about how my life had maybe finally begun, after a few delays. I was still young. I could buy a bicycle and never take the subway again. I could take out student loans that I'd never repay. I could mail a picture of myself with long hair and smooth skin to my mother. I could forgive Violet and then methodically have sex with all of her friends, never let her touch me again.

At the end of the dishes, there was an empty sink. I watched the water run down the drain for a moment.

"Thank you," Adelaide said quietly from behind me. When I turned to look at her I noticed for the first time a weary expression on her face.

"No worries," I said, and meant it.

I turned off the faucet and looked around for something else to do.

Separate Ways

My new bedroom — upstairs, down a narrow hallway, next to the bathroom — was completely empty, except for the small stack of boxes in one corner. Its emptiness was a provocation, a template for a room more than a room. It was supposed to be filled with comforts, materials, plans.

The third day, Erin came over. When she left in the morning, long before it had become light outside, I didn't argue or ask her to stay. She murmured something to me about having somewhere to be, and could I call her after class, maybe we could do something fun? I think she thought I was asleep, so it was like she was talking to herself. She went on and on, getting amused and then frustrated by my lack of response. She always said I didn't listen, so I'm sure this didn't feel all that unusual to her.

I heard the bedroom door close. A few seconds later, the slam of the heavy front door. I got up.

Sometimes I imagined people from school talking about me. I imagined them in apartments in far-flung cities passing over my name in casual conversation, the last, *Huh, I wonder what happened to her*, tapering off into a final, *I literally have no idea*. It felt like rebirth, in a way.

Erin and I had had sex in the new bedroom, which had been weird. The second time we ever had sex, years ago now, was in the fourth floor bathroom of the linguistics building, which had been weird in the same way. Places empty of associations but carrying the stains of long human use, adding to a silent ledger, the building's mute memory. Lesbian sex between two eighteen-year-olds in a stall that smelled like chemical cleanliness and urine.

In my room there was the yellowing gray carpet on the floor, and the white walls studded with little pinprick holes that used to have thumbtacks and nails in them.

I opened the window and went back out to the sloped roof, blinking at the beginnings of the blue morning light. The air smelled like pine and decay and truck exhaust, and it carried some dampness that promised rain. The previous day I had removed the lopsided, broken Venetian blinds dangling over the windows and left them in a heap on the curb. From the roof, I looked down at where they lay, covered with yellow maple leaves from the neighbor's tree.

When I unpacked my books, I found an old chapbook of Lawrence Ferlinghetti's *Pictures of the Gone World* I had gotten for a dollar at a bookstore in Chicago. I opened it to the first poem and remembered reading it years earlier. "Away above a harborful of caulkless houses / among the charley noble chimney-pots of a rooftop rigged with clotheslines / a woman pastes up sails upon the wind."

That was a woman, perpetually appearing from behind something, too busy being a part of the world to consider it from the outside. She was the soft pink inside of the world.

Back when I got it, I had just noticed the beauty of the poem's imagery. Looking at it now, it had an added weight. I wanted to be outside the world, like a poet, and I wanted to be inside the world, like a woman.

I thought about putting my books on the curb, next to the blinds, for old women and students to sift through on their walks. Instead, I put them in the empty spaces on Lauren's bookshelf. Most of my books were thin little poetry collections, unobtrusive next to Lauren's thick, cracked-spine novels.

I went in, closed the window, and cautiously went down the stairs to the living room. In the silent, gray morning, I noticed details. There were two panes of stained glass in the little windows, so even when it was overcast, the light made the inside look warm. The faint rectangles of pink and green light lay above the front door, on the kitchen cabinets, on the tile backsplash below them. I read the envelopes of junk mail on the kitchen table. There was a novel by Heinrich Böll (*The Bread of Those Early Years*) face down on the love seat by the window, next to an abandoned tarot spread. The Emperor, the Hermit, the Five of Wands. A big stack of faded board games on the floor next to the bookshelf, the dull-colored ceramic bowls Lauren's recovery sponsor made that were full of stones from the beach in California. One on the coffee table, one in the kitchen next to the stand mixer.

Lauren woke up early, around six-thirty, when I had already been up for a while, writing in my diary at the kitchen table. She turned on all the lights, put on an apron over her ruffled linen shirt and jean shorts. She was already wearing her work clothes.

After she got some stuff sizzling in a pan, she rifled through the CDs stacked next to the player in the kitchen and picked one. A slithery clarinet struck up a familiar, easygoing dance with a string quartet.

I recognized this one. Mozart, Clarinet Quintet in A. Memory is peculiar, I had that one down to the key it was played in. Lauren probably didn't know that, but she knew a lot of other things about music that I didn't know, knew so much that it made me wonder where she had picked it up. Lauren could talk about classical music with Erin for hours. They'd say things like, *The late quartets of Beethoven*, and throw German and Italian words at each other. Comparisons, meta-concepts of music; composers, conductors, soloists, "pieces."

I looked up from my diary and watched her stir eggs in the big cast iron pan. A fat, shiny carabiner dangled off one of her belt loops on the left side of her hips, just below where the band of her underwear was visible — a white line of elastic with a thin red stripe running through it. She hadn't shaved her face or plucked her eyebrows in what had to have been at least a few days — there was a faint smear of mascara below her left eye that seemed to extend one of her dark circles into the space between her nose and her cheekbone. I realized that I could just about decide which version of her I wanted to see, shifting her under my eyes. Boy Lauren, Girl Lauren. I shooed that thought away.

She brought two plates over to the table — over-medium eggs and green salsa balanced over strips of fried corn tortillas. That and two mugs of coffee.

"Did Erin already leave?" she said.

"Yeah," I said. "This is nice of you, by the way."

"I make this, like, at least once a week," she said through a mouthful of it. "It's, like, automatic for me."

"Thank you," I mumbled. It was delicious, filling and warming. I let myself finish the whole plate.

"Amine told me you're the easiest move he's helped with," Lauren said. "He was like, 'she lives like a monk,'" she said.

"I do," I said simply.

She looked at me strangely but then returned to her plate. You don't want to talk that much that early in the morning, with the long walk to work fixed ahead of you in your mind. When we finished she took the plates to the sink and refilled my coffee. Her back flexed as she moved a sponge in a circle around the plates, and then the pan. The dishes done, she poured the rest of the coffee into a Thermos and walked over to the window, gingerly took a half-full pipe of weed off the sill.

She opened the window with one hand and exhaled smoke out of it. I went to sit by her on the windowsill, pulled my knees up to my chest, and looked out into the burgeoning morning. Our building cast blue shadows on the garages on the opposite side of the street. When I looked at her, I saw some concern in her eyes. I wondered what she saw in mine.

"I gotta go," she said, after a few quick hits of the sour-smelling pipe. "If you don't need help setting up, wanna come visit me when I'm done with work?"

"Sure," I said. "Erin said she wanted to hang out."

"Ok," Lauren said. "Does Erin like me?" she added.

"Why wouldn't she?" I asked.

"She has her guard up around me," she said. "It's just how it is, I guess. It's like she doesn't want me to see the creepy way she treats you."

I made myself smile, cocked my head to one side. "She's not my girlfriend," I said.

"That much is clear to me," she said.

"You know she's calling herself bisexual now," I said.

Lauren scoffed. "You know what I think about this," she said, dismounting from the windowsill. She started rummaging through her bag, making sure she had everything. Then she ran into the bathroom to wash her face.

"See you later," I said, retreating to my room.

"Cya," Lauren said crisply, covering her face with shaving cream.

※

Everyone calls this place "charming," and I guess I get it. People who come from the college town a couple miles away like the old houses, the old trees, the new coffee shops and restaurants in the center of town, the open space. They like it because they can live cheaply in a beautiful little town, and they hadn't really considered living in the middle of nowhere before. The town has a name that makes people in cities scrunch up their faces in inquiry. *Is that near Detroit?* It is, but if it weren't for the highway that hummed constantly in the background, we could be miles and miles away from anything real. Those people come to this place, they come to nowhere, and they say, *This seems nice and quiet.* It is. Poverty and obsolescence tend to be quiet.

Erin and I both grew up in narrow brick houses near the highway in Detroit that smelled like cat piss and cigarette smoke. She had spent her childhood summers going up north, and the first time I went over to her house in high school she showed me pictures of her shooting guns. No one at school thought she was a lesbian, the way they were somehow able to sniff that on me. They just thought she was snobbish, which she was. But I could see something else there, or wanted to, and maybe that was why we became friends. We kissed for the first time a week after graduation, and then a week later we had sex in the backseat of her parents' car in the parking lot of our high school.

In college, my infatuation for her became a scab I kept ripping off. I rationalized it to myself when she'd only sleep with me when she was sad and feeling vulnerable. I told myself that she wasn't being cruel when she told me about boyfriends, about going home for Christmas, when she'd still try to get in bed with me after getting drunk. She meted out attention casually, sporadically, and just as suddenly would ignore me.

I spent my time laying around in my room, thinking about nearly nothing. Or, I'd walk around. I was still figuring out what to do here. I needed a job, and I needed a project. Erin had a project. She was in school to prove it. I thought about going over to Erin's house, to see if she was back from class yet. She'd probably be sitting at the piano next to the big windows in front of her huge yard. When she wasn't in front of a piano she was irritated, distracted. In her last year of undergrad, when she had gotten her own practice room, she'd make me sit outside if I was early to meet her. The narrow hallways in the basement of the music school were full of people playing their instruments beautifully, acrobatically, repetitively. From Erin's room, I would hear explosions of upright piano punctuated by long silences. "You can leave if you want," she'd say, in the doorway, not letting me in. "I'm in the middle of something here."

Erin had a project, and that meant her time was really just the time between now and her death, measured into days that she drank down like tall glasses of clear, cold water. *I shouldn't be greedy. I'll see her later. Don't you have anything to do?* The familiar self-reproach, like an echo of all the times before when I had hoped.

Hope was over now. I needed something firmer than that. I wasn't sure where I was supposed to look for it. In myself, to start with.

I put the remaining cardboard boxes from my move — containing clothes I didn't want to wear, sentimental trinkets of little value, unserious decorations — in the closet and shut the door. Then it was almost four, so I could go see Lauren.

≋

Lauren was the first trans woman I had met. I had seen them around on the street in Chicago, but here they were just friends with my friends. A month ago, Erin and I had gotten stoned on the roof of her house, and she had monologued for a long time about Lauren, whom we had both just met.

"They look more confident than women do," Erin had said. "It's the most interesting thing about them."

"Cis women," I said automatically.

"Sure, whatever," Erin said, waving her hand. "They're living examples of repudiation, you know. You just look at them, and you know they know what it means to be a man, and they see that it's a sham."

"Lauren is confident," I offered.

"She's got herself figured out," Erin said.

"Do you think she'd say that?"

"I'm saying it," Erin said. "She's reached her level."

Living example. Someone's visible queerness made them an exemplar of some vague idea of spiritual commitment — that was Erin, who was probably straight after all. That was when I had realized it. I didn't say anything, but I felt protective of

Lauren in that moment, my new friend, who was older and wiser and could surely save me.

The superiority I felt over Erin was only of this kind, the knowledge that I wasn't lying to myself. It didn't really help. Most of the time, my queer friends told me to stop tormenting myself, to cut her off without warning or apology. Lauren was the only one who understood that I had a *problem*, not a temporary daze I could be awakened from; she was the only one who understood that my problem was the same as my hope. I got into the habit of going to meet Lauren behind the Vietnamese restaurant where she worked, and we'd go on walks. When I walked and talked with her, she'd help me examine things. With her, I was worldly and outward and unconcerned with my inner life, unless it could be reduced to a set of syllogisms. We were going to figure out the secrets of desire together, in a way that gave me a welcome reprieve from experiencing it. She listened to me endlessly. Now that I lived with her, I wasn't sure if either of us wanted to reprise the roles we knew to put on for each other.

I went behind the squat restaurant in the strip mall opposite the river and she came out the back door with a cigarette dangling from her mouth, untying her apron. Behind her, there was a clamor of dishes, industrial sinks, and people shouting to each other. She closed the door and the sound faded.

"How was work?"

"Shitty," she said matter-of-factly. "You have any job interviews lined up yet?"

"Working on it," I lied.

"Cool. I wish I was unemployed. I don't, but, you know, I do. Wanna go to Frog Island Park?"

I nodded.

We walked through the small downtown area, near the old train crossing. Main Street is just behind the tracks over there. I think every town has a Main Street. Parking lots next to old, old three-story buildings with arched windows, storefronts on the first floor. Some bars and restaurants with stray figures eating in the big windows. If this area went on and on instead of terminating at the river bridge, it could be a city. A strange kind of antique city, a city of emptiness where people somehow still lived.

As we walked, Lauren listed a bunch of places I could work. The anarchist bookstore, some of the coffee shops. The university a long bus route away, which always needed recent graduates to fill out paperwork. She said she knows someone who studied English and works in a greenhouse now, and offered to give me their phone number.

"You're quiet," she said as we descended the long, wide concrete path to the park, which was covered in tall, weedy grasses and the frail, dead stalks of dandelions and ragweed, burdocks and mulleins here and there, curious and warped sentinels.

"I guess," I said.

We alighted on a picnic bench near the bend in the river, next to a big cottonwood tree that had already shed all its leaves.

"Is something going on?" she said. "You seem sort of distant."

"I don't know," I said. "Mostly it's just the same old stuff."

"Sure thing," she said.

From her bag Lauren produced a Ziploc of weed and a grinder, a water bottle, and her little purple sketchbook. She rolled a joint on the sketchbook and handed it to me. While I lit it, she opened the sketchbook and looked over at me, moving her pen over the page.

"Can I draw you?" she said.

"Sure," I said, handing the joint back. She balanced the notebook on her knee so she could keep drawing while inhaling.

"I'm thinking of calling things off with Erin," I said.

"Oh, *yay*," she said, not looking up. "Aren't we seeing her tonight?"

"I don't know," I said.

"Sounds like you don't want to," she said.

"I don't know," I repeated.

"What changed?" she said. "Like, I'm curious what led to that decision."

"I have limited time on Earth," I said.

She looked up at me and smiled. When she smiled, even with the makeup on, I noticed the laugh lines running back from the corners of her eyes up to her temples. She was thirty-three, but she looked both older and younger.

"That you do," she said.

※

Tomorrow, Erin texted, much later. Just the one word. That meant her mind was in a knot that couldn't get undone until some bars of music had revealed themselves in their forbidding, dissonant perfection.

You got it, I texted back. I fell asleep like I always did, quickly and into a nothingness without dreams.

※

In the morning, Lauren was gone, but she had left the sketch she made of me at the park on the coffee table. It was my face, round and cratered, with the big eyebrows, my hair tied back. In the picture I didn't look vexed or troubled at all. I looked happy.

※

The next day, Saturday, I met Erin over at the same park. The sun was bright. She was sitting at the same picnic bench I had sat at with Lauren the day before, fiddling with an old digital camcorder.

"Hi," I said.

She looked up and waved. "Hi. One sec, do you mind if I shoot some video? I'm behind on a piece."

"You make video now?"

"No. I'll explain later. Here," she said, standing up. "Don't mind me."

She got off the bench and walked over to the river and waded into the shallow, silty part near the bend. She aimed the camera at the water.

"How's the new place?" she said.

"It's good," I said.

"Mm," she said. She aimed the camcorder up at the trees. "How's living with Lauren?"

"It's good. We both wake up really early."

"Good," she said, putting the camcorder down and facing me. "I've been trying to get up earlier. I don't know how you do it. Here, that's all I needed. C'mon, let's go back to mine."

"Sure."

We walked back up to Main Street. She didn't look in the storefront windows. Eventually, we got to the alley that cut between two tall green buildings. Behind the unpainted brick backside of the Main Street row, with its boxy protrusions and wooden fire escapes, there were long rows of one-story garages and shacks, painted white. One of them had a hole in the roof. She led me to the biggest garage, tucked behind a crooked tree, and unlocked a door next to it. This building belonged to her composition teacher, who was renting it to her for cheaper than it was worth.

She grabbed a hold of my hand and led me through the entryway to the big main room. Twenty-foot ceilings, brick walls, casement windows on one side of the room, an upright piano in the corner next to the windows, stuffed bookcases and piles of CDs and records. In the center of the room, there was a huge trestle table with her desktop computer, some synthesizers, and a pair of expensive speakers. It was like a temple to music. Having Erin around all these years, I knew about a whole other province of experience, one I could never satisfactorily play the right part in. What was new was a big projector screen installed on one side of the room. I loved this room, and wanted to get a good look at it for the last time.

"I have to work, unforch," she said. "But I can still talk."

"Totally," I said. "What's all this?"

"Here, lemme show you."

She clicked around on the computer until some ancient-looking software filled it. She pressed the space bar and the projector screen lit up with a rapid montage of images and snippets of video, none longer than a few seconds. Videos of Erin moving a hand over her bare breasts, archival footage of dynamite exploding on a black-and-white hill, videos of places in town that I recognized.

"It's a piece for piano and video track," she said, leaning over the computer screen, dragging and dropping things. "I'm still figuring out the relationship between sound and image I want to have."

"Huh," I said.

"Huh," she mimicked me in a high-pitched girly voice, not looking up.

I sat in the broken chair a few feet behind her, in front of the overflowing closet. She looped through parts of the video. I couldn't say anything intelligent about what she was doing, as always, and I didn't want to ask her questions.

"Should I go?" I said.

"No," she said. "Talk to me."

"About what?"

She swiveled around in her seat. "What's *with* you?"

"If you're busy, I can leave," I said.

I had a habit of averting my eyes in front of Erin's gaze. Looking at her straight in the face took a little bit of effort, even when we were making love. Those blue eyes, like nets of bright color spreading outward from her pupils.

"Suit yourself," she said. "I'll be done in, like, an hour. We can get dinner afterward maybe."

"I don't think I can do this anymore," I said.

She turned around again, then stood up, which I hadn't expected.

"What do you mean?"

I stood up too. She closed the distance between us and reached a hand toward my face. I didn't stop her. She brushed some of my hair out of my eyes. It was always her prelude to a kiss.

I responded a little bit, tilting my head up. Then I took a step back.

"What's up?" she sighed.

"I think I want this to be a relationship," I said. "You don't."

"I — "

"You *don't*." I was surprised by the intensity in my voice. "Like, I think you think that this is normal, but that's the problem. It's been years of this — "

"That's unfair," she said, before I could continue. "God, this is just like you. You don't *talk* to me about this stuff, and then — you know, I'm not a mind reader here. If there was something about our — "

"I'm *leaving*," I said. "This isn't a conversation."

I didn't move, though. I searched her face for information. I was holding on a little longer than I had to. If she had said something with love, I might have faltered. But her look was her usual steely impatience. Behind us, the screen flickered between different images, seemingly stuck on a short loop. Water — trees — water — trees.

"Is that it?" she said incredulously.

"Yeah," I said.

I got up and left. The light outside was golden and dazzling. She followed me to the doorway.

"I'm *sorry*," she said from the doorway. She said it with spite, like it was just something else she was burdening me with, which it was.

"Yeah, okay," I said, and kept walking.

≋

When I got home, I found a pair of fabric scissors in a can of markers and pencils under the coffee table. I sat on the floor in front of the full-length mirror by the door and watched myself cut off the big strand of hair that hung down on one side of my face. Never again would Erin tuck it behind my ear. I cut off the same piece on the other side.

I had started, so I had to keep going, keep cutting. I looked worse and worse the more I did it. I laughed at my own reflection, then I started crying.

The invective voice I had used against myself, ever since I was a teenager, came easily to me. *You ugly, dumb girl, you can't take care of yourself. You'll always lay the blame for your own life on other people. The real people take on the weight of the world, they take and take and take.* I said some of this out loud, and it made me feel better.

When Lauren got back from work, I was still sitting there, holding the scissors in one hand, like a child. I saw her expression go from concerned to amused in the mirror.

"Girl, what the hell did you do?" Lauren said from behind me.

"I'm done with Erin," I said.

"Thank god. Here, I used to cut hair when I lived in the Bay. Let me fix this."

She sat on the floor behind me, took the scissors out of my hands, and brushed out my hair with her fingers. After a moment's pause, she started to add small snips around my grand gestures. Eventually, she nudged me to sit down in one of the kitchen chairs.

I got used to Lauren's hands moving my head around. I closed my eyes and almost fell asleep.

Do-over

As my mom recounted it, my dad didn't expect to get nearly everything when his mother died. I surmise that his brothers didn't take it very well, but there was nothing for them to do — the old house and the majority of the money and investments went to him, the rest of her savings and a few mementos were parceled off to them.

The last time I had been at that house was Christmas before I moved east. When I was a teenager, the house had seemed unfathomably and forbiddingly grand, like something out of a nineteenth-century novel, but by then I dreaded going there. At dinner everyone would listen to my dad's bombastic, self-aggrandizing monologue about his business, while my hick uncles — general contractors or store managers or IT guys in Saline and Milan and Pinckney — would all wait and listen until they could interject with corollaries. Their shrewish, bottle-blonde wives and my sullen cousins stayed silent. My dad was the one who was being enterprising, taking some risks, so his words were worth the most of anyone there.

My grandmother sat at the head of the table and didn't speak either — her silence was imperial, not cowed; she'd watch us watching Dad, sipping from a narrow glass of port, almost seeming to look past our present selves and seeing the children we all once were. She was quietly satisfied to have all her progeny and their wives there, even if none of them had especially amounted to much, but she was also scrutinizing us, withholding judgment until the end.

That last Christmas, my grandmother cornered me after dinner. The men and childless women were milling around in the grand front parlor, drinking and pacing and talking. She was already beginning to lose her lucidity by that point.

"Kieran," she said. "I hope your father is doing all right."

"He is, I think," I said.

"With all this with his work," she said, leaning in close to me, moving her hands, "I just hope he doesn't lose sight of himself."

She was talking so quietly I had to bend down to listen to her. She wore an imploring look I often saw on her face in her old age. "Sure," I said.

"I just," she said, then paused and grimaced before starting again. "I just don't want him to go the way of your uncle James."

I nodded solemnly.

"You know, Kieran," she said, gathering confidence, "In this life, a lot of people will try to convince you that you can't be. That you can't do. And if you run into trouble, you know, that confirms it. You just need to know that you can do great things. And I mean you too."

She looked up into my eyes, and then her head seemed to droop like a flower toward my enormous feet in torn-up sneakers and her black leather clogs. At a loss for words, I nodded again and patted her on the back. It was a condescending, dismissive gesture, but I really couldn't imagine what response she wanted.

I knew about my dad's business problems, of course. He was a few feet away, talking loudly and amiably with my uncles close by the drink cart. He didn't seem convinced that he "couldn't do" at all, but she had seen him in his shaky, confused adolescence and doubtlessly had something of a broader perspective than I had.

His business filed for bankruptcy four months later. For months afterward, he was unreachable. I went by his one-story house on the north side of Ann Arbor and his car was gone. I looked in the big front window and all the furniture was moved around, pictures on the walls were askew, but no dishes out or any overt mess. The TV was gone, and the bookshelves were empty. No outward signs of catastrophe, he just wasn't there. My mom refused to talk about it, which I guess was her right as a woman who had been divorced for a decade.

The bitterness was getting to me. I had to leave. After I moved east, it started to seem possible that I would never see him again. He started to become more of an idea to me than a reality. I would remember things he said to me but not his face. I stopped returning calls from family, and never got any from him.

I hadn't known how quickly your horizons can contract, until it feels like you're running directly toward a blank, black wall with no clear knowledge of even where you're coming from.

Toward the end of my experiment in Philadelphia, strung out and staring at the ceiling of the one-room apartment I shared with Marian, I started thinking about my past — less specific thoughts or even feelings, more a vague recall of images appearing one after the other in non-chronological succession. The image-memories couldn't conjure up emotion — I was beyond that — but I couldn't forget them. They would shimmer in front of me, superimposed on the unforeseen failures every day would bring. There, staring at the ceiling, I would monologue about it to the empty air, or to Marian, who was unresponsive. I'd open the window to let the freezing cold air in and feel sorry for myself.

※

My mom moved to a nicer place in Ann Arbor sometime in the last couple years, one of those neighborhoods where the professors and doctors live. It's got two floors and a guesthouse at the end of the driveway, over the garage. The guesthouse is more like a cabin, or an extension of the garage — snug and insulated, but a lot of exposed wood. It's got enough room for a sink, a bed, and a desk. That's where I'm staying now, until I figure out what's next.

It was full of leftover things from when my mom's friend, fresh from divorce, had used it as an art studio while living in a tiny rental nearby. Paintbrushes, thinner, solvents, used palettes all piled in a corner. She'd bike there in the morning and leave a tiny painting in my mom's mailbox at night before she left, about the size and shape of a halved envelope. Most of them were paintings of animals — a giraffe, a koala, a manatee. My mom had arranged them above the desk. To this I added a strand of Christmas lights and a pile of clothes and CDs on the floor. On the desk, I put a shoebox full of everything I needed to do my estrogen shot once a week, with the dwindling supply I got Marian's friend to get me back in Philly. A full-length mirror in the shape of a truncated oval leaned against it.

Maybe the third day after I got back, I did my first estrogen shot since getting out of the facility. I came back from taking a shower in the house and ruffled the towel through my hair, which was almost down to my shoulders. At the desk, I pressed play on the little CD player on the desk, and Sonic Youth's *NYC Ghosts & Flowers* started playing somewhere in the middle of the record from the built-in speakers. I got out the syringe and the drawing needle and the little vial and the little bottle of rubbing alcohol.

I always looked away when I stuck the needle in — I guided it into my left thigh as I glanced up out the window, to where the streetlight across the street illuminated the branches of the neighbor's black walnut tree in a mess of half-outlines. Then, the blush of sensation spreading down from the injection point, not pain exactly but a heightening of awareness of the insides of my leg.

I put on an XXL t-shirt with the logo of a singer-songwriter on it that I had cut up into a tank top, with twin slashes underneath the armpits. It hung down to my knees. Under it,

I wore a periwinkle sports bra, which was too tight around my rib cage. A girl at the facility had given it to me — it conferred no real support, but I liked that it was visible when viewed from the side.

There I was, in the oval-shaped mirror, with the hollow face and the clothes borrowed from women and never returned. I look like what I am, I thought. I sat on the balls of my feet on the floor in front of the mirror and started mouthing along to Thurston Moore's laconic, demented monologue under the muttering guitars. I moved my hips in a slow circle, I put my hand between my legs and made a slow pulling motion toward my belly button. I imagined bass tones moving through my body, articulating it for me, vibrating through the floorboards.

I shuffled over to the CD player on my desk and pressed stop before the next track started. I went to look in the mirror again. My skin was less sallow and looked softer. I tried a smile but it came out looking strained. Marian's friend told me the effects of the estrogen would be mostly psychological, and I believed her, at least initially, but I wasn't sure what that meant, what was supposed to change.

I went back to the desk and looked out the window again, above the koala and the giraffe and the manatee. The night was all deep, deep blues. I was up late sitting like that, waiting for the memory parade to wind down.

〰

I woke up at around nine with a text from my mom: *Your father's been calling all morning, can you come talk to him?*

I stood in the living room in my pajamas and dialed the number my mom had written on an index card. She had retreated to her office already, turning around to notice me but just nodding as I walked to the phone. She closed the door.

He answered on the first ring. His voice was too loud. "Kieran! God, I truly didn't know WHAT had — "

I winced. "Hi, Dad. How are you?"

I could hear the sound of traffic behind him. "I'm good! I'm good. We should catch up sometime. Your mom told me you're still lookin' for work, so I bet you got free time. But guess what. I'm workin' for myself again, so my schedule is wide open. Name the time, name the place."

"Um. Are you doing anything right now?"

"Nope! You?"

"No," I said. "I just got up. Uh, you wanna, like, go to the Fleetwood?"

"Sure!"

"Okay. In an hour?"

I shaved my face and practically ran out of the house. I took a table on the patio, watching cars pause at the intersection before speeding off. When he got there he looked the same, save for the white hair where his dark brown mane used to be.

He grinned when he saw me, and when I stood up to shake his hand he hugged me.

"Kieran! Oh, Kieran. It's so good to see you," he said, before letting go and slapping me on the shoulder.

While he was inside ordering, I poked at my phone, methodically marking texts from people in Philly as *read* and deleting a few for good measure. Every time I looked at my phone and saw the texts piled up — apologies, pleas, solicitations — I felt sick. They had stopped coming in about a week before I got my phone back.

He came back, followed by the waitress, a tall woman with a smoker's voice and hair dyed neon red.

"Coffee for both of ya."

"You're an angel," he said.

"I get that a lot," she said. "Hey, I remember you," she said, looking at me.

"I used to come here in high school," I said.

"Oh yeahhhh. You used to look different, but ya can't fool me. You'd be here in the middle of the damn night with what's-her-name with the crazy hair, really *poofy*." She placed her hands at a distance from her head to illustrate. "I still see her sometimes."

That had been so long ago that it took me a second. Difficult to even think of that version of me as the same person, but to someone the waitress's age it must have felt like last week. Being reminded of that time was jarring, uncomfortable, but I recovered quickly.

"Hanin, yeah," I said. "She still lives here?"

"Sure thing," she said. "Used to work at the Kroger's on Maple. I think she's up in Ypsi now, haven't seen as much of her."

"I just got back. Maybe I'll run into her," I said.

"Maybe so. Where ya been, hon?" she said.

"Philadelphia, mostly."

"Ahhh. The City of Brotherly Love. Love that place. I got a cousin out there, used to visit him sometimes. He was the smart one in our family. Used to drive my uncle crazy. Well, I'll see ya, I'm sure."

A motorcycle went by a few streets away, sending a loud, flatulent noise echoing through the still-quiet streets. She had gotten me thinking about that time in my life, had made it real again. I made a mental note to come back and ask her about Stephanie, Joe Kowalski, Zack Harris, and whoever else seemed likely to remain around here. That seemed more approachable than calling anyone up. Who knew if they still had the same phone numbers, anyway, and who knew if I wanted to see anyone again. My dad smiled and stared into his coffee, waited for the door to close.

"So where the hell have you been?" he said in a quiet, pointed voice, almost a whisper, looking at me imploringly across the table.

I moved the spoon around in the coffee cup. "Mom didn't tell you?"

"No. She doesn't tell me *anything*."

I sighed. "Can this wait until later? Or just ask her."

"Sure thing," he said. "I'm glad you're okay, is all. I started askin' after you with your friends — you know Mike? That guy you were buds with in high school? I worked with him at Stella's Bakery out in Ypsi."

My stomach dropped. "I didn't know you worked at Stella's."

"Oh god, I'm glad I got my break when I did. That was gonna kill me. It's all right if you're, you know, how old are you?"

"Twenty-four."

"Twenty-four. My god, I'm nearly fifty. I'm too old to be making bread all day."

I nodded politely, unsure how to respond.

Our food came out a few minutes later — a long, wide plate of hash browns covered with vegetables and feta cheese for me, pancakes for him.

"Enjoy, guys," the waitress said, ducking back inside.

"I never understood the appeal of that," he said, as I covered the plate in hot sauce and ketchup.

"Haven't you ever been stoned at three in the morning?" I said jokingly, taking a sip of coffee.

He looked at me somberly.

"Okay, okay, okay, fine, not the time," I said, focusing on moving things around on my plate. "What have you been up to?" I asked.

He leaned back in his seat, clearly about to begin one of his speeches. "So, as you probably know, your grandmother died," he said.

He always said *your* when describing our mutual relatives to me. He wouldn't say *my mother died*. "I heard," I said nonchalantly, putting my fork in my mouth. "I was never close with her, and, y'know, I kind of fell off the map."

"Yes, you did." He shifted in his seat before continuing. "So, she left me the house on the west side, as well as a bit of money."

"That huge brick thing? Are you gonna move in?" I was trying to sound offhand, unbothered, independent.

"No. Once I get the approval from the zoning board, I'm gonna turn it into a business."

"So that's what you meant by 'working for yourself.' What have you been doing in the meantime?"

"Right now I'm guttin' it," he said. "Takin' all the furniture out. I'm payin' my friend Irv to help cart her shit out, do an estate sale out of a warehouse in Ypsilanti. Easier that way. Half of it is expensive and half of it's worthless. We got a huge dumpster in her driveway right now. I think between what she left me and the profit from the sale, I can set up a bike store."

My mouth was full of hash browns. I nodded for him to continue.

He was getting animated. "I learned how to fix a bike when I lived out in Ypsi, right? Because I was so broke that I couldn't afford a car. And my bike was so busted, I had to keep goin' on YouTube over and over to figure out how to fix *this* thing and *that* thing and the *other* thing. Lord, that was a tough year. Bikin' everywhere and bakin' bread. But y'know, I learned to fix anything that could break on a bike. Eventually, I started fixing my friends' bikes for, y'know, money for beer, or just as a favor. And I got a reputation."

I could see it so clearly. There were places like this all over Ann Arbor — some old house built in eighteen-whatever, transformed by the ceaseless creative industry of the local eccentrics into ethically-sourced coffee shops, disorganized record stores, one-man musical instrument repair operations, boutiques for off-brand Wolverine merch ("Harvard: The Michigan of the East" "Ann Arbor: Ten Square Miles Surrounded by Reality"). He was going to become a member of The Local Community again, the only way he knew how. What he was telling me was just a rough draft of what he was going to tell the journalist for the *Ann Arbor Observer*. It was like he was looking straight through me into the future.

I took a sip of water before continuing to attack the hash browns. "So why not open the shop in Ypsi?" I said with my mouth full.

"I *love* that old house, but it's too much for me to live in," he said. "Y'know, I think your grandmother thought I would remarry, but I'm too old now."

"Gotcha."

"I'm gonna convert the top floor into an apartment, nice and spartan," he said. "Hey," he continued, looking at me across the table (he hadn't touched his food). "Your mom said you're lookin' for work. Why don't ya work for me? I'll pay you fifteen an hour to haul all her shit out of the house and fix up the place, and then you can work for me once business gets goin'."

Obviously, this was what it was working up to. "Sure, I guess," I said evenly. "Only for a bit, though. I'm moving soon."

"No worries!" he said, grinning. "I'd love to have ya. It'll keep you out of trouble."

I raised my eyebrows. He didn't seem to notice.

"Tomorrow at seven," he said. "I'll see you there?"

I looked at him. "Sure."

He cut himself a big piece of pancake and shoved it into his mouth. "Deal," he said with his mouth full, and extended his hand across the table for a handshake.

≈

I walked there the next morning. The door was propped open with a cinder block, and I could hear the sound of a drill from inside. I stood at the foot of the staircase that led up to the slightly sagging porch and placed my hand on the worn railing.

The sound of the drill stopped and I heard heavy footfalls on the wooden floor. A woman emerged out onto the porch with a pack of cigarettes in her hand. She had hair shorter than mine and was wearing the same beige cargo shorts and white t-shirt I was, although of course they looked better on her. She looked at me curiously.

"Oh, are you Steve's son? Here," she said. She turned around and grabbed a tool belt from a milk crate next to the door. "He's not here today. This is yours. You're gonna need some gloves, too, maybe better pants, and some boots."

"Hi," I said, taking the tool belt from her. "What's your name?"

"Irvine. You're Kieran, right?"

I remembered that Dad had said Irv at breakfast. "Uh, everyone calls me K," I said, on a whim.

"Your dad doesn't call you that," she said matter-of-factly. She lit a cigarette and pushed her bangs out of her face. She didn't wait for my response. "Ever worked with your hands before, K?"

"Not really."

"That'll be ok for now. We're just movin' things out today."

"Ok."

I stood there, waiting for her to finish smoking. She gestured to the spot next to her on the porch. I sat down next to her.

"So, uh, how do you know him?"

"I was his manager at Stella's in Ypsilanti. Good guy, really reliable, never had trouble with him, y'know? When he got this crazy windfall inheritance, he asked if I wanted to work for him, 'cause I have some experience with, like, construction and remodeling. I'm handy. He literally never shut up about the bike shop for the last, like, four months." She had a high, scratchy little voice.

"For sure," I said.

She stubbed the cigarette out on the sole of her work boot and tossed it into the yard. "This must be weird for you," she said. "Given that it's your grandmother's house and all."

"Not really," I said. "I was never here much."

"Sure," she said. "Wanna get started?"

We went inside. The living room was unrecognizable — boxes everywhere, furniture turned over, curtains pooled on the floor by the windows. It looked like she had been in the process of disassembling a table comprised of four thick slabs of varnished wood holding up a thick lacquered top. That was it, that was my grandmother's table. Huh.

"It's a shame about this thing," she said, gesturing to it. "But I think your dad was pretty firm that no one would want it. Also, it's heavy as a motherfucker. Here, you can take these bits I've already taken off of it to the dumpster out back. I printed out the list of stuff we're keeping, and we're getting rid of the rest. You mind if I play some music?"

"Not at all," I said quietly.

She fiddled with her phone, and a few bars of chorused guitar started playing from a Bluetooth speaker on the floor. A woman started singing.

"What's this?" I said.

"My friend's band," she said. "C'mon, let's get started."

It took about a week. My dad didn't appear at all, but sometimes we'd see him when we drove stuff to the showroom outside of town where he was hosting the "estate sale." He had rented a small space in one corner. Four or five other showings would be happening simultaneously, which explained why we were trashing so much stuff. Every morning at Grandma's house, Irvine would stand in the doorway to each room, a hand on her hip, checking the printed-out spreadsheet my dad had compiled, and then we would load the van with valuables before throwing everything else out — rugs, curtains, trinkets, books, photo albums, pictures in frames.

My odd grandmother, someone I never really knew, who had been born to a farming family near the Michigan-Ohio border in the 1930s, who had lived to be nearly ninety years old, who bankrolled half this town while she was alive. I imagined her sitting at her usual place at the head of the table, sipping that glass of port, as she watched two queers grunting and sweating while reducing her Edith Wharton house to a collection of walls and windows.

At the end of each workday I was usually physically exhausted and in a mental haze that wouldn't fade until I had gotten back to the guesthouse and lay down for an hour or so. Irvine, who never lost steam during the workday, was even more energetic, as if hauling heavy objects and boxes of miscellany out of the house had pumped her up. A couple times she'd walk with me on my way home and pepper me with questions.

"So you live with your mom?"

"Yeah."

"How's that?"

"It's alright."

She fished the pack of Marlboro reds out of the pocket of her overalls and lit one.

"Just alright?" she said.

"Yeah," I said.

"If you'd rather I leave, it's chill," she said, exhaling a huge cloud of smoke. "But I figured I don't know anything about you besides that you're Steve's son and that you're sober."

"You don't have to leave," I said. "And, like, what else is there?"

She sort of snorted. "There's gotta be more," she said. "You're twenty-four. That's long enough to have something."

I noticed, for the first time, how incongruous we looked in this neighborhood. On this walk in my sweat-soaked work clothes, I passed men wearing polo shirts and women wearing crisp white blouses walking shampooed dogs, leading drooling children by the hand. I tried to think of what to say and came up with nothing.

"Alright," Irvine said when the silence extended out for a little longer. "I get it. You can't get rid of me, though. Tomorrow, bright and early."

She walked backwards in the opposite direction I was going for a few paces as she said this, and gave me a two-fingered salute.

Something like this happened a couple more times after work. I knew that I should have engaged a bit with the person I spent the most time with out of anyone, I knew that Irvine could probably help me, or at least see me clearly if I told her the truth, but it felt a little beyond my abilities, like a shelf that was slightly out of reach.

When we were done emptying the house, we went to drop off the truck at my dad's apartment in Ypsilanti, and he answered the door in a robe.

"Good work, guys," he said. "Kieran, you want to spend the day together? Celebrate a little?" He sounded woozy, like he had just woken up. I looked curiously into the space behind him in the apartment.

"I can drive him," Irvine said quickly.

"Sure, sure," he said. "Thanks again. I'll see you Monday."

We didn't talk much as she drove down Washtenaw in the quickly fading light. We hadn't talked a ton during the week and just knew surface-level information about each other. I wasn't sure if she knew about my situation in any detail, what my dad had told her. I wondered how the two of them had become friends while working at the bakery.

"Oh, nice," she said, looking at her phone at a stoplight. "My roommates, Steph and Hanin, are making a frittata tonight, so I get to go home and just, like, immediately have food."

I paused. "Your roommate isn't named Hanin Abi-Karim, is she?"

"*They* are. You know them?"

"Oh, shit, yeah, I didn't know."

"No worries. How do you know them?"

"Uh, high school. I know Steph, too, if it's the same Steph I'm thinking of."

"Oh shit, no way. You should come over sometime."

I couldn't really imagine myself doing that. It was an interesting thought, but what would I say to them? I found myself thinking about it anyway, playing out the scenario in my head. The last time I had seen Steph and Hanin, we were in some backyard in Kerrytown smoking cigarettes and talking about our post-grad plans. I was trying to disguise the fact that I sort of didn't have any. They would be unsurprised to see that I hadn't amounted to anything, probably.

"Yeah, sure," I said, maybe unconvincingly. She didn't bring it up again the rest of the way home.

When she dropped me off at Mom's house, she gave me a peace sign as she was backing out of the driveway. That felt familiar, if not exactly friendly. It was something, and maybe it would lead somewhere. I had someone in the world who knew me again.

≈

A team of electricians came in to rewire the place and install track lighting on the ceilings of the tall living room. Then, over the next two months, Dad and Irvine and I covered two of the brick walls with drywall, painted the walls a neutral gray-green, drilled holes in the wall for bike racks, built shelves and a countertop, rebuilt the porch from scratch, replaced doors, and put a big metal sign above the door that read "STEVE'S BICYCLES BOUTIQUE AND REPAIR." Then, we sanded and refinished the floors. Every day Dad would show up with a detailed list of instructions, and we'd stay until everything was done — sometimes a few hours, sometimes until nearly midnight. Dad would drive me home every night after work, so the abortive conversations with Irvine didn't happen again.

At times it felt like we were ruining the house that used to awe me with its beauty and gracefulness, but I was prevented from feeling this by Dad's laser-like focus on the day's tasks. Whatever we showed up to do, he only wanted to focus on that, and didn't want to talk about much else.

It felt appropriate that I was back to do this. Ann Arbor felt at times like a figment of my imagination, suspended permanently in the state it was in since I left, and it felt good to destroy something that used to matter. My back started to hurt.

I learned new words — *gauge, rating, epoxy, sealant, structural integrity*. There was a science to this, an unforgiving battle with the laws of physics. Every stroke of the hammer had a context and a rationale, which Dad would explain to us at length, squinting at his phone in the living room, before we did anything. He would sometimes end up arguing with Irvine about the details while I stood there, uncomprehending, waiting for orders. Once or twice, Irvine lost her temper with him.

"Steve. Steve," she said, loudly enough to get him to pause in the middle of his monologue, "I know you've researched this, but I have to tell you — I've literally *done* this exact thing, in a building a *lot* like this one — "

I was surprised by her vehemence. She was basically shouting at him, gesturing with both hands. I looked down at my boots.

"You can call your brother, you can call him *right* now," she went on. "Tell Dale what you *just* told me, you ask him if that's a good idea. It'll never pass inspection that way, and that'll set us back *weeks*. It's not worth saving a couple hundred bucks."

He had his hand on his hip and a tight, furrowed expression on his face. He squinted at his phone again, as if double-checking, and then looked back up.

"Alright," he said. "You win, Irv. You go take Kieran to go get those materials you *say* you need."

"*Thank* you," she spat, and stormed out. I heard the truck start in the driveway.

"God, what a headache," he said, running his hand over his face. "That's why I have her," he continued, resignedly. Then, as if he just remembered that I was there, he looked up and me and snapped, "What are you doin' just standin' there? Go get in the truck."

Irvine didn't seem upset when we were driving to Home Depot. "God, your dad is stubborn," was all she said. "He always sees reason in the end, though."

"He's always been that way," I offered.

"I bet you know that better than I do."

"I've never seen anyone — challenge him like that," I said.

We were at a stoplight. She rolled down the window and lit a cigarette. "I mean, I'm not his kid. And I was a woman working construction, y'know? I know how to talk to guys like that."

I wanted to ask her how she had ended up doing that, but I realized it was the wrong question. She probably didn't have an answer either.

After we crossed through downtown, we drove for a few blocks through the long, low-slung warehouses in the Fingerle Lumber Yard, near the field where the marching band practiced.

"It's crazy that this place is still here," she said. "This place used to be a hangout spot when I was in high school. I'd come here at night with friends, with girls."

"When was that?" I said. I realized I didn't know how old Irvine was.

"Mm, twenty-ten or so," she said. "Did people go there when you were in school?"

"Yeah, in college too," I said. "Then they installed those floodlights."

"Mm, yeah. Less appealing after that, I bet."

I was thinking about a night a few years ago, early September, nearly blackout drunk and throwing empty glass bottles at the side of one of those buildings, one after another, until I heard a police siren and ran. I didn't remember what I was angry about, I just remembered anger, uncontrollable and impossible to disobey. It was hard to imagine that was the same person.

"This is prime real estate," Irvine mused. "I bet it isn't even profitable anymore. The university is gonna buy this whole place up in five years and build something shiny."

≋

It had been ninety degrees all week but it finally cooled off that night. I was often restless after I got home. I was rummaging around in my mom's house for snacks past midnight and she came out into the living room. I froze.

"Kieran. Sorry, you didn't wake me up, I have a horrible headache. Could you get some chamomile started for me?"

As the tea was steeping, she sat at the little breakfast table by the bay windows. She looked ghostly in her nightgown, her hair hanging in a stringy curtain around her face.

I hadn't seen much of her that summer. We'd cross paths in the morning but only briefly, her eating breakfast while I was already halfway out the door in my work clothes. Like me, she was an insomniac, so we'd have the greater part of our conversations at night. During the day she was all business, but at night we remembered that we had things to say to each other.

"I drove past Grandma Betty's today," she said.

"Mm."

"I can't believe he's really doing all that. The house he grew up in."

She shook her head and looked down at the table, her hair covering her face. She massaged her temples.

"It's coming along well," I offered.

"Sure. I mean, all of his schemes always start out well. At least you're not invested in his success. Is he paying you on time?"

"Yeah."

I handed her the tea and sat across from her. She straightened her back and took a sip.

"And what's next for you?" she said.

"I don't know," I said.

"Well, I like having you here," she said. "But you can't stay forever."

"I know."

"You have a degree from a good school, you're smart — I don't know, Kieran. You can't work for that man forever."

She was using the tone of voice she had honed from decades of talking to brash young students. It served to place an impassible barrier between us. It was disconcerting how easily she switched into that voice. I wanted to remind her that I was her — daughter, whatever.

"I could," I said.

"I'm sorry," she said. Then, after a long pause: "I shouldn't try to press you. You're in — you're in a transitional moment right now, and I should respect that."

I nodded. The air in the house felt heavy.

"I should probably go to bed," I said. "I had a long day today."

She nodded. I went out the back door.

By the end of the summer, the person in the guesthouse mirror looked strong and lithe. Still rail-thin but not junkie-thin, corded arms and a four-pack and legs suddenly lineated with fresh definition in unexpected places. Small, barely-there breasts, longer hair, eyes that were slightly less sunken into their sockets.

I tried some names on in the mirror. Kiera, Katie, Kathy. I didn't want a big change, just a couple phonemes nudged around. I decided that I didn't have to decide now.

When she wasn't jabbering with my dad about the construction details, Irvine was pretty quiet. She played all sorts of music while we worked, and never seemed annoyed when I always asked her what it was, but that was never the pretense for a conversation, just information she gave me, like what kind of screw to use for a bracket.

After we finished building the porch and put the sign up, the city inspector came by — a stern-looking Black guy with a clipboard loaded with papers. While he went inside, we all sat in lawn chairs and drank iced coffee.

"This was all just the three of you?" he said when he emerged from the house. We all stood up.

"Yes sir," Dad said.

"Huh," he said. "Well, I have some notes, and I'm gonna write up a report. But the short answer is, you passed."

Irvine smiled. I hadn't seen her do that too often.

After he left, Dad took the truck on one of his interminable errands, and Irvine and I were left to our own devices. It was the middle of a hot, humid day. She leaned against the side of the house and fixed me with the same amused look she had on our walks.

"Hanin and Steph want to see you, by the way," she said once the truck was out of sight. "They told me no one knew where you were for a while."

"Yeah, I was sort of AWOL," I said.

She gave me a weird look, then it faded and she continued: "If you're not doing anything right now, I think they're both at Riverside Park in Ypsilanti. I bet we could go meet them there."

"I think I can't," I said.

"Laaaaame. What else were you gonna do? C'mon, come see your old friends."

She was right, it would be lame not to go. I didn't argue much after that. We got into Irvine's car, which was full of junk. She rolled all the windows down and blasted Xiu Xiu as she chain-smoked her way down Washtenaw, rarely dipping below the speed limit.

"They're telling me they're in the river," Irvine said, looking at her phone at a stoplight. "Hmm. I might swing by the house and grab my swim stuff, if you want?"

She pulled up to a small, squat house with a gravel driveway. She opened the door.

"Here, I have a spare pair of trunks, come in and you can change."

Their apartment, in the first floor of the house, was a small, tidy space. Big couches in the front room, a full bookshelf, a record player. Irvine ducked into her bedroom. I caught a glimpse around her. There was a big double mattress on the gray-carpeted floor. The rest of her stuff appeared to be on the floor too. She closed the door and came out in a pair of black swim trunks and a blue, loose-fitting swim shirt. She tossed me a pair of red trunks, which I changed into in the bathroom.

When I was a kid, my mom talked about Ypsilanti like it was a dangerous other world, somewhere it was a misfortune to go. I learned later that it's not like that at all, of course. It's a lot more human than the genteel place Ann Arbor is becoming. In the summer it has an overgrown quality. People let all sorts of bushes grow wild right up to their big, utilitarian porches and leave the lower limbs of trees to grab at pedestrians' heads. Riverside Park — a shallow, sandy bend of the Huron River wrapped around a finger of swampy land — was never touched by a lawnmower, let alone a landscape architect. In the summer it turned into a shady meadow with a couple picnic benches here and there as an afterthought, burdock and wild carrot and mulleins and black-eyed Susans bursting out of holes in the mud.

When we got there, Steph and Hanin were all sitting on rocks half-submerged in the river up to their chests, drinking beer. Hanin had shaved their head and Steph had grown her inky black hair really long, but otherwise they looked the same. I tried to identify evidence of weathering on their faces and saw a little but not too much. We were all still young, after all.

"Look who I have," Irvine said as she walked up.

"Is that Kieran Reynolds??" Hanin shouted, standing up as I walked toward the riverbank. They splashed out of the river and embraced me, leaving spots of water on my t-shirt.

"God, it's been a fucking minute. How are you?"

"I'm ok," I managed.

"C'mon, it's too hot to stand in the sun," they said, gesturing to a pile of shirts and backpacks. "You can put your stuff there."

I deposited my shoes in the pile and then, after hesitating, pulled off my shirt, scampered into the river and found a rock in a deeper spot of the river that hid me up to my waist. Irvine's swim trunks billowed under me with the current.

I was sitting next to Steph. I turned and said hi.

She looked me up and down. "'Sup, Kieran. Or — K?" She looked at me inquisitively.

"Uh, either's fine."

"For sure. So what's new with you?"

I contemplated putting my head underwater instead of answering. "Well, um, I just moved back to Ann Arbor. I'm working for my dad right now, and — "

"Ahhh, cool. You went to Michigan, right? What for again?"

"Yeah. Um, I did a double major in English literature and sociology."

"Mm. You were in — Philly? New York?"

"I lived in New York for a bit and then I moved to Philly with my, um, I guess you'd say ex-girlfriend. And now I'm here."

"Gotcha, gotcha." I tried to make a furtive glance down at my chest seem casual. She noticed, or I thought she did.

"What are your pronouns, by the way?" she said, casual as ever. "Irv called you K, but is it like the letter, or like C-A-Y? Sorry for just calling you Kieran out of the gate."

"Um. Yeah, I'm not too public about it, but I go by Cay now. Like, the second one. And uh, like, they/them I guess? Or she/her if you want to."

She seemed nonplussed. "Word. It's nice to see you, Cay."

It was a spur-of-the-moment decision. (I've been Cay ever since.) Steph continued asking me questions:

"Are you gonna stick around here?"

"Probably not, I just needed, um, I just needed a break."

She sighed. "I'm on break, I guess, too."

She went on to update me on her life: She was working in an office at EMU; before that she worked for U of M at the vast labs on the north side as an assistant to a chemist — she was hoping to go to graduate school the following year, but had been summarily fired when the chemist was denied tenure. She still wanted to go to grad school, and named a long list of institutions where people were working on what she was working on, but was disillusioned with academia following her firing. She told me that she was just hoping to get to a better place with her mental health — she had been diagnosed with BPD at about the same time she had been fired — before she could think about her future. I nodded along.

Hanin splashed over and offered their gloss on the situation (that everyone who worked in academia was selfish and that it wasn't worth it). "Hi Kieran, by the way," they said.

"Find me a place where I can do science all day that isn't graduate school or, like, the military," Steph said, clearly irritated by the interruption. "And she goes by Cay now."

"Oh, my bad," Hanin said. "Jesus, dude. Like, duh. I'm trans now, too, how about that."

"I hear it's because they're putting chemicals into the water," I said. Steph laughed a little too loud and long.

"Something like that," Hanin said. "I'm assuming we're going back to the apartment after this, right?"

"It's a day off," Irvine said. She had her eyes closed and was in the water all the way up to her neck. Just her small, pale face was poking up from the swirling, sandy water. "Where else are we gonna go?"

≋

Steph and Hanin and I were never really close friends, to tell you the truth. I mostly knew them through other people. The diner waitress had remembered one or two times, not much more than that. It was like I had never disappeared, like I had just gone around the corner and was back with them on a sidewalk in Ypsilanti after a short absence, making polite talk and waiting for everyone else to join us. But this was all there was left, maybe. I started to feel a little washed-up, talking to Steph on the way back.

On the porch was a stack of milk crates with a lighter and an ashtray on top. Four broken-looking wooden chairs surrounded it. I nervously sat in the one closest to the door. Hanin started rolling a joint and continued a conversation with Irvine, speaking quietly enough that Steph and I couldn't hear.

"Did Irvine show you any of her comics?" Steph said, lighting a cigarette.

"No," I said.

"She's really good at it," Steph said. "She used to make her own paper. Like, she'd make pulp out of paper bags and old receipts and stuff."

"Huh," I said.

"Her comics were about these two aliens," Steph said. "One with four eyes and one with five eyes. And it was never clear if they were like, dating, or if they were just friends who had sex."

"I guess it's a subtle distinction," I said.

"They, like, argued about it in the comic," Steph said. "You know, it sort of paralleled a relationship Irvine was having with this girl who couldn't commit."

"I know how that is," I said vaguely.

Hanin passed me the joint. I took an ambitious hit and suppressed some coughs. Irvine looked over at me and raised her eyebrows. I met her eyes and took a second hit, then passed it to Steph, who was still explaining Irvine's comics about the lesbian aliens. The joint went around the circle again, and by the time I had hit it again I was floating a little away from myself, barely listening to Steph's monologue.

"We're going over to Jean's place," Hanin was saying suddenly. Them and Irvine had stood up. "They're gonna shoot off fireworks."

"It's not even July anymore," Steph said meekly, already following them.

As we walked a couple blocks to Jean's house, Hanin and Irvine walked in front of Steph and I, so I couldn't help watching Irvine. Staring a stoned stare at her. It dawned on me that she wasn't really all that stoic, that was just her work persona. Here, her voice was an octave higher, she talked with her hands, and at one point she giggled when Hanin got to a good part of their story.

"How was your time in New York and Philly?" Steph said from next to me.

"Sort of boring," I said, not looking at her. "I was addicted to drugs."

"Sure," she said gently. I think she expected me to keep going. I started to tune in to Irvine's conversation with Hanin.

"Steve is an *ally*," Hanin was saying, laden with sarcasm.

Irvine turned around and smiled at me. "Sorry to be talking about your dad right in front of you, Cay," she said. "I was just telling them that I think he, like, understands my gender in a way? Like, he holds doors open for me, but he also says, 'what's up, *duuuude*,' whenever I see him."

"He does that to me too," I said.

Hanin laughed. "Okay, that's a demerit on his ally card. But I'm assuming you're not out to him?"

"No," I said. "That one is on me."

"It's not on you," Steph said, with a motherly sweetness. She was reassuring me. "It's not your fault," she added.

"I think in this case, it is," Hanin said, and returned to their conversation with Irvine.

"Coming out is hard," Steph said. She tossed her cigarette butt into the street and lit another one immediately.

"I bet it is," I said.

When we got to Jean's house, we cut around it into a little gravel alley ringed with garages. Two women with big, frizzy hair and a lot of tattoos on their bare arms were sitting in lawn chairs there.

After some introductions, Steph and I sat down together in the gravel and watched Jean and Irvine fiddle with bottle rockets.

"Welcome to my home," Jean said. "I promise I'm not always doing this sort of bullshit."

"More often than not," Hanin said.

"I singed my eyebrows off with one of those things when I was, like, twelve," Steph said.

"How did you even do that?" Irvine said. "I feel like the first rule with these things is, like, you run away from them."

It was clear to me that Steph didn't know how much to look at me. She kept glancing up directly at my face and just as quickly moving away. I noticed the slope of her shoulders, her protruding collarbone. I found myself looking away too.

At some point Irvine broke off and looked at me with a serious face. She inclined her head away from the circle and I walked with her to a spot a few feet away.

"Hey," she said quietly. "Like, I figure weed isn't the thing you were in rehab for, but your dad told me specifically to keep an eye out for you and drugs, and so, like — "

There was that "your" again, the same one Dad had used when talking about his dead mother in the diner. Your dad. My employer. I watched her trail off and start waving her hands in frustration. I guess weed makes some people anxious.

"Yeah, I won't tell him," I said.

"Okay, I mean — that isn't what I meant, I mean, I didn't do something bad, did I? By giving it to you?"

"It's fine," I said.

"Okay," she said, looking at me with a serious expression. "Okay."

We got back to the circle.

"Nice night, huh?" Steph said.

"Yeah," I said.

When I looked back at Steph, she was looking at me, and when neither of us looked away, she leaned in and kissed me.

I wasn't sure how long it was going to last. It lasted a while. I remembered how much I liked kissing girls. This time it was a little different — Steph took the lead, leaned way in, bit my lip a little bit. She placed her hand above my belt and a little to the left. On my waist, I guess that was my waist. She started drooling all over my face. I wondered if Irvine was watching. I sort of hoped she was. I felt vaguely like I was proving some kind of point to her. Eventually, Steph pulled away from me and wiped her hand on her mouth.

She giggled and leaned into me once she had lit another cigarette.

"Cute," she said approvingly. "Nice to have you back."

Irvine was looking everywhere but me. Then Jean lit the bottle rockets and we all looked up into the sky.

Ponytail

It was an unseasonably warm day in February, and I was walking through slushy sidewalks to the train station after work with three of my coworkers. Two of them were talking to each other about EBT.

"I mean, two-fifty a month — I'm not *starving* without it or anything, but that's the difference between being able to, like, make the food I want to eat, and not being able to."

"Right, like, I don't have to be constantly doing math in my head."

Sara was short and femme and had pink hair, Fern had been taking low-dose testosterone for six months, Rebecca had jet-black hair and bangs that hovered high and skeptical above her thin eyebrows. And then there was me, the only trans girl in the group, just sort of towering over them. We formed some piece of the inevitable scenery in the part of Brooklyn centered around Broadway and Myrtle, doubtlessly connected in some people's minds with raising rents and the encroachment of cafés like the one we worked at, which in addition to overpriced coffee also sold a random assortment of books, dried flowers, crystals, tarot decks, incense, and so on.

When we got back to the apartment it was about eight and it was pitch dark outside. Rebecca reheated some leftovers and disappeared into her bedroom for the evening, flicking on the lamp that scattered pink light around her room before closing the door with her foot. I ate some crackers and arranged myself in front of my mirror. I heard the beginnings of some HBO show through the wall as I did my makeup, and then she found her headphones.

It's taken a year of living here, but I think I finally like my bedroom. It's narrow — my queen-sized bed takes up most of it, and the only other piece of furniture is a small table with a big mirror with lights around the rim. I found it on the street a while ago — obviously, the lights didn't work, which is why it was on the street, but those can be fixed with a soldering iron, a few trips to the hardware store, and some patience. I had one window, with bars over it, that gave a good view of the brick row houses with arched windows and beautiful tall stoops on Wyckoff Avenue. I had hung a translucent purple curtain over it, which fluttered a bit because I always kept the window open just a crack, even in the gross, wet winters. When I sat there, my face brilliantly illuminated, with the sounds of the street filtering up into my little, cell-like room, I felt calm and protected in the way a bird must feel in the ample knot of a great tree.

I took a little orange pill — Adderall XR, 20 mg — from the bottle I kept in the drawer of the vanity. I considered taking two, but it wasn't going to be that kind of night. A visit to a meaningful ex, then a house party, no afters. I had to be at my best, but one was enough.

Then, clothes. I slid open the door to my closet, which was overflowing with stuff I got from sample sales and online. Clothes are my one serious vice. I couldn't afford to buy any of this stuff new, obviously, and even buying it resale made dents in my bank account I struggled to justify to myself. But, you know, being trans, you have to put in a lot more effort to be taken seriously, or that was what I told myself. After some deliberation I chose an Eckhaus Latta top with an opalescent, sequined texture like fish scales, and some high-waisted black pants I had thrifted and tailored to add pleats around the hips. Over top of it, a green leather trench coat. This would turn heads, I thought, angling my body in my mirror, feeling slightly giddy as the amphetamines kicked in.

An hour later I was standing in front of a row house on Bedford, shivering. It had gotten colder and somehow damper, and it felt like the streets were being scooped out by wind. The door opened.

"Come in, come in," Ambrose said before I could even see his face clearly. I followed him as he scampered up the steps.

The first time I met him was at a party uptown, back when neither of us had transitioned yet. He was wearing a white lace dress, and had his eyes closed and was spinning in circles around a stripper pole installed into the middle of a living room floor. I walked up to him and placed my hands on his shoulders, and he stopped, opened his eyes, and looked up at me.

The eight months we dated were disastrous for both of us. We were both mentally ill and violently in denial about being trans. We wanted to preserve our sense of being normal, functional, heterosexual, preprofessional; when that didn't work out, we resorted to becoming codependent, talking about getting married, having bigger and bigger fights, clinging and clawing at each other like the proverbial drowning people. Finally, one night he stabbed me in the arm with a fountain pen and I had to get it removed in the ER. He went with me and apologized the whole time. When I got discharged at four in the morning, I finally just told him that I needed to not see him for a long time, and that he should lose my number. He sputtered and wailed on the street, his long red hair plastered to his face with snot. He said *I love you I love you I love you* over and over and it felt like he was stabbing me again. I walked away from him, feeling weightless, not sure how I was supposed to feel beyond that I was "making the right decision."

Two years passed. We maintained sporadic contact as the two of us separately transitioned and moved to Brooklyn, aware of each other in the archipelago of queer friend groups that were offshoots of the same queer friend groups from when we were in school. Then, one day, he texted me.

I sorted through my feelings and decided that I wanted to see him. I had forgiven him by that point — I guess by then I thought about the things he did less as "ways he hurt me" and more like biographical data. Both of us had in all likelihood spent long hours processing the relationship, which I knew was formative for both of us, talking about it with friends and therapists and subsequent partners. Then, probably, we had started to think about it again, in a somewhat different light, once both of us made the difficult decision to transition.

I couldn't tease him, or lie to him, or try to smooth over anything, the way I might have when I was younger. Those were the games college kids played; we had to be, at minimum, honest with each other now.

I looked up at his ass as he led me up the stairs to his apartment. It was the same ass, just in bigger pants. This reassured me.

His new apartment turned out to be completely empty except for a standing desk, a bike, a cat tree, and a precarious stack of books next to the standing desk, which just had his laptop and laptop charger on it. The light came down harsh and flat from the overhead lights. There weren't even any boxes or anything. I heard him clatter around in the kitchen.

I sat on a patch of floor near the tall window on one side of the room. Through it, I could just make out the flickering lights of the Williamsburg Bridge from around a taller, newer building.

He came over to me with two negronis in wide, squat glasses. I indulged in checking him out. His face seemed to have gotten wider and more solid, and he had a little dusting of facial hair the same red as his buzz cut. His shoulders and arms had a new layer of dense, corded muscle, and when he pulled up the sleeve of his oversized striped shirt I traced the path of a vein up his forearm into his tricep with my eyes.

We had texted, so it wasn't tense. I asked him why his apartment was so empty and he said nonchalantly that he was thinking about it as a sort of "spiritual project," but also that his bookshelf, books, and table were at the apartment he used to share with Julie in Bed-Stuy. Julie had stopped responding to his texts. It sounded like he had explained this a lot of times before, and I could tell he didn't want to talk about it.

After that was clarified, he asked me some very literal questions about my life. I told him:

1. That I live with Rebecca Travers and her girlfriend,
2. That yes, that means I see the quote-unquote "lesbian poets" around a lot, Rebecca being one of them,
3. That I work at that bookstore slash café where Rebecca was a manager. That yes, it's an okay gig, one where, thank god, I was allowed to sit down while working a cash register and a computer with BookScan installed on it,
4. That I'm not seeing anyone, but mostly because I'm not trying, mostly because I feel like I'm in an "interim period" in my life. That transitioning made me warier about the intentions of potential partners, and that yes, that's kind of not ideal, but, like I said, interim period,
5. That yes, I know a lot more trans people now, definitely more than in school, but yeah, "queer community" is such a fucked concept, if you think about it, which I have.

In return, he told me:

1. After he broke up with Julie he started dating a cis man who made a lot of money and who was evidently a fetishist who was stringing him along,
2. This was obliquely related to Julie not giving him his furniture back — something about "boundaries," about "disclosure," about going to "get thrown around by some guy who smelled like dude sweat and cologne" (his words) and then getting in the same bed with his lesbian ex. Ambrose thought Julie "felt threatened" by him "exploring his sexuality" at all, despite the fact that he was always bisexual. This factors out to some kind of transphobia, apparently,

3. Julie was giving him the silent treatment, as were a host of her friends, presumably about his weird conduct after they broke up. He'd sort of been persona-non-grata'd in some dyke circles because of what happened there, which he said was "unfortunate," but will "probably only last a few months,"
4. He had some work from home data-analyst job now. "Tech trans, you know," he said. I did know, but I hadn't met one. I just assumed they lived in, like, a different part of the city entirely or something, or had somehow managed to upload themselves to Twitter and Reddit. Also, that they were all girls. "Not all of us," he said. "I'm trying to become the first male girlboss." I could tell that he had rehearsed the joke or probably said it before.

During all of this catching-up we drank two negronis each, at one point relocating to the kitchen (also empty — one set of dishes, no chairs) so he could make another round. After we had got the basic stuff out of the way, we were sort of at a loss. We lingered in the kitchen, him leaning against the countertop, me sitting on the windowsill next to a radiator. I sipped my third drink. I watched him staring at my breasts, which felt like the most sincere compliment he could give me.

"Yeah, I guess in sum, my life is pretty boring," I said.

"Boring's good," he said, swiveling his head around as if just noticing the blankness of his apartment for the first time. "Boring means nothing's going wrong."

I raised my glass. It was almost irritating how comfortable I felt around him. It was like resuming the good parts of our relationship, as if nothing had happened, we had just traded genders and turned down the volume on the neuroticism. The physical distance between us felt good. I could plausibly keep him at exactly this length from me. He would be forever in the same room with me, but six feet apart. It was just as well that his life now seemed perfectly self-contained, finally stabilized. He had no room for me in it. Perhaps uncharacteristically, I was prepared for that, and I was happy for him.

Twenty minutes later we were in the train station and he was explaining the party we were going to for "maybe an hour." He told me it would be "mostly Columbia people," even though most of them had graduated by now and doubtlessly had jobs, lives, other contexts.

He sounded somehow less enthusiastic about it than I was. "We won't have to stay for that long," he said. "But it'll be good to see everyone, you know?"

Since we both graduated, he had been hanging around all these people we both knew in college, but had recently started to seem unhappy about his newfound status of visible minority among them. It's not like we were going to be the only emissaries from queer Brooklyn at this party, but, y'know, he used to be just another smart girl. Now, who knows?

That's the thing about transitioning in your twenties, I guess; you start changing a lot right when everyone you used to know starts learning the fine art of staying put. I thought about saying this to him but thought better of it.

We got off the train in Queens. The blocks we walked through were strangely nonspecific in their character — low garages, row houses, and boxy office buildings interspersed with blank lots and suburban-looking New England houses. We finally arrived at an unassuming-looking three-story brick building on a long block of identical buildings. He texted someone to let us in.

The first thing you saw when going into that apartment was a large, beautiful circular mirror in a brass frame right next to the door. I watched my reflection as I let Ambrose take my coat off my bare shoulders. The mirror was so clean and polished it almost seemed to glow. Or maybe that was me glowing. Not to brag, but I looked really fucking good, and I was happy in a dumb unfeminist way to have a guy there to take my coat off at this fancy party.

Ambrose darted off, promising to get me a drink. I gradually came to understand that this apartment took up the entire first floor of the building and had the size and shape of a detached house in the suburbs. The different functions of an apartment weren't all jammed on top of each other the way I was used to. The furniture was understated, and it all went together. Dub techno played from speakers on the floor. I automatically started comparing my taste to the taste of the hostesses. What would I have done differently, if I had this kind of money? This was usually a way I blunted my envy, but in this case it was hard to think of something I could improve on here. There was nothing yuppieish about it, nothing that suggested received ideas or clichés. I spent a while just standing in the entryway, swaying a bit as I carefully took in the scene.

The first people I saw, I knew pretty well, mostly from college. There were a few additions, partners and plus-ones. They had all mostly figured out how to turn their expensive degrees into careers that paid dividends in some way, be it money or clout or prestige. The guy in the brown shirt just got back from a year-long sojourn in Mexico, and the woman he was talking to was a semi-prominent cultural journalist who wrote about TikTok trends or something. There were a couple sad-faced people in the middle of law school or PhDs, and there were a few people who didn't seem to do anything. I liked these people, despite myself. They bolstered my conviction that you can't be all that interesting if you're just another insider.

In the kitchen I ran into Yvette, one of the hostesses, an actually talented writer for whom this party was undoubtedly just a fun little distraction. She was leaning against the countertop, disinterestedly watching a guy in a white t-shirt doing a line of coke off a mirrored tray with a pewter frame. I walked up to her.

"Hey," I said.

Her face lit up. "Veronica, hi," she said, hugging me.

The music was loud, and I missed a lot of what she said to me at first. We had to shout to be heard.

"This place is so fucking cool," I said. I proceeded to list off the virtues of the furniture, the decorations, the location, the music, the mirror by the front door, the appropriateness and good taste she had, her outfit.

"I feel like this is a good place to put down some roots," she said, deflecting my compliments. "I love it out here. It finally feels like I have a home."

"Do you own this place?"

"Rachel and I co-own it. Ambrose said it was like a 'Boston marriage' kind of situation. We're just best friends who are like, soulmates."

"That's beautiful," I said sincerely. "I haven't seen you for a fucking year," I added.

"We have to catch up some time," she agreed, then she tapped me on my shoulder and darted off.

Ambrose finally caught up to me with a glass of wine.

"This place is like, so nice," he said.

"An actual *glass* for wine at a house party," I agreed. I inclined my head to the back door and he nodded. I fished in the pockets of my pants and found my little weed pen. The Adderall was hitting a little too hard; I had been more manic than I had intended with Yvette. I needed to cool off.

It was raining a little, but there was an ample awning over the door to the backyard. To my mild surprise, there were two trans girls out there smoking cigarettes. Ambrose seemed to know them.

"Wow, all the trans people are all outside to smoke, how *original*," one of them said.

"This is just like Metro," the other said.

I tried to recognize them as transmuted versions of guys I knew from college. They were both super early in transition, like less than a year probably, and dressed in a way that they probably thought was "dykey" but was really just unflattering and semi-closeted. Whenever I saw girls like that I wanted to take them downtown and force them to max out their credit cards. There's only so much you can do with clothes and hair and makeup, but some people aren't even trying.

"Veronica, you know Tristan and Esmé," Ambrose said.

I did, I remembered now. Huh, wouldn't have guessed. "Hi," I said. "You both look great."

"I love your outfit," Tristan cooed. She was looking at me like she wanted to eat me.

"Thanks," I said. I heard my voice come out crisp and neat on the syllable. I took a big rip from my weed pen.

"Can I have a hit of that?" Esmé said.

"Sure." I handed it to her.

"Okay, me next, and then I have to go inside," Ambrose said. He hadn't brought his jacket. "I'm freezing."

Esmé took two indulgently lengthy pulls on the pen and then handed it to Ambrose, who took a dainty little sip and then handed it to Tristan.

When he was gone, Tristan and Esmé looked at each other and smirked. Tristan hit the pen again and then passed it to Esmé.

"Didn't think I'd run into *him* here," Esmé said.

"I'm shocked he didn't call us *dolls*," Tristan said.

"He loves that word," Esmé agreed. "It helps him feel like he has a chance with us."

"It really completes the picture," Tristan said. "You know, with the way he dresses, and the voice."

"The voice?" I said pointedly. I felt suddenly protective of him. They hadn't given me back my weed pen yet for what I decided was too long.

"Yeah, you know," Tristan said. "The like, Humphrey Bogart impression. It's worse when he's drunk. I find it especially funny because he sounds like a gay little *Muppet*, so it only sort of works."

"It works on someone," Tristan said. "Straight girls," she added dismissively.

"I mean, like, hypothetically, if I were a trans guy," Esmé said, "I would have so many different gender expressions to choose from. And *that* was the one he went with."

"Oh my god. Are we being mean?" Tristan said.

"He's an abusive shithead, I don't care," Esmé said.

"Yeah," Tristan agreed. "How've you been, V?" Tristan said.

I reached out and snatched the weed pen from her hand as she was in the middle of making some stupid hand gesture with it, and then I went back inside without saying anything.

The word *abusive* had completed the picture for me — *that* was what justified the gross, transphobic way they felt empowered to talk about him. Was it possible they were thinking about *me*, that those girls believed they were saying all that on *my* behalf? I didn't really know where that story had ended up in the endless game of telephone that the "trans community" played with other people's lives.

The other possibility, that those girls knew something I didn't, and that he had caused some hurt somewhere outside of the people in this room, was significantly worse. I didn't think he was capable of physically harming someone; this would inevitably be something murkier. I suddenly remembered the crass way he had talked about his ex-girlfriend earlier that night. Was it *that*? Had he been hiding details, subtly shifting the emphasis around? If I asked him about it more pointedly, and I would have to, he would have some countervailing story that partially exonerated him. And it would be *true*, or at least a version of the truth. That was the worst part. If he hurt someone else in the way he hurt *me*, it would require time to sort through. God knows I had to sort through it. I'd have to weigh the evidence, and then I'd have to take sides, because queers always make you take sides.

I'd wanted to let him back into my life because I had been very fond of him at one point. Then again, I had dumped him when I realized that his good intentions, his love, his admiration hadn't prevented him from being a fountain of problems for me. Maybe I should have just stuck to that.

I took a lengthy, contemplative rip of the pen in the kitchen. I should have just gone out to the backyard again and asked those dorks what the fuck was up, but I was sure I would hear it from someone else. It was probably inevitable, actually.

A guy in the kitchen tried to engage me in conversation and I ducked to a quieter part of the room. I discreetly checked my bank account and decided I couldn't get away with calling a car. I wondered how long I'd have to wait on the windy M train platform to get home, how much longer I'd have to wait if I stayed for another hour.

Fuck it, I thought, looking around at this room full of people suffering from an overabundance of options. *I got what I needed out of this.* I found the table with the liquor bottles and took a shot of bourbon, and then I made a lap toward the door.

I wanted to think about anything else. In the entryway, a woman and a man were halfway out the door with cigarettes in their mouths. The woman got my attention because I didn't recognize her at all. She was wearing an outfit that should have made no sense but was actually sort of perfect. Her dress was made out of pale orange satin, and over top of it was another dress that was like a loose net that hung at an asymmetrical angle. Her boots were leather and went up to her knees. She pulled on the *perfect* coat over this ensemble. Unlike mine, hers actually looked warm enough for the weather.

Just at first glance, she was the most interesting person I had seen all night. I put my coat and shoes on and followed them out the door.

"Hey there," she said as I opened the door. It was fully raining now, and the two of them were crowded under the awning.

"Shit, can I bum a cigarette?" I said. I was slurring my words a little bit. When did I become such a lightweight?

"Of *course* you can," the girl said, reaching a hand into her purse. She went on talking to the man, who I also didn't recognize. "Here. So, yeah, after term ends I'm flying out, but the surgery doesn't happen for another couple weeks. It's nice that I was able to get someone in the Bay Area, I guess, you know, right by my parents' place in SF. And I told myself that I'd do another dissertation chapter in that time, 'cause

I'm gonna be, you know, recovering for the next month after that. I have it all planned out, I have all the sources arranged. It's just a matter of putting words on paper."

Surgery. Oh, got it. If her face hadn't given her away, her voice would have. You could tell that it was a distinct choice on her part to keep the tenor and male resonance, but make the most of it nevertheless. Silky and bright and utterly distinctive.

"I feel that," the guy said. "I mean, not in the sense where I'm getting my face peeled back in two months. The putting words on paper part."

"Yeah? How's the novel coming along?"

Something about how the guy talked about FFS irritated me. The way he emphasized the word *peeled*. I wanted to shove him, or say something cutting and appropriate.

"Are you going to Dr. Thomas?" I blurted out. That was the wrong thing to say, but I could recover from that.

"Wow, *clocked*," she said, blowing a cloud of smoke directly at me. "Yes, I am."

"I had a consult with him last year. I'm on his waitlist," I lied.

"Nice. I mean, half the girls I know went to him," she said. "He's got a good reputation."

"On that note, shouldn't you be not smoking?" the guy next to her said.

"Ugh! I have another *month* before I need to stop. I'm *tapering off*."

"What's your name?" I asked.

"Huh? Oh. Arabelle. Bella."

Arabelle. Jesus Christ.

"Veronica," I said.

"I'm Dustin," said the guy.

"Congrats on the surgery," I said.

That was wrong too. "Congrats." As if it was a raise or something. There's no formal etiquette for this stuff, but you always know when you mess it up.

"*Thank* you," Arabelle said in a way that evinced zero gratitude.

She was looking at me with an amused smirk on her face that made me inwardly flinch a little. It was *thrilling* to meet someone else who seemed genuinely indifferent to the polite atmosphere of solidarity "we" are supposed to have, but I did wish she made an effort to talk to me. We probably weren't that different, although as I looked her up and down again I realized that she was wearing like, at minimum, fifteen hundred dollars worth of clothes while talking about writing a dissertation.

I sensed an opening in the way Dustin was looking at me. He was scanning me up and down. I decided to play a little dirty:

"One thing about Thomas is that he gives all the girls the same nose," I said casually.

"What's the nose?" Dustin said.

"You've seen it," I said confidently. "*Real Housewives*, you know. A little button with a ski jump. No one is born with a nose like that."

"I haven't noticed," Arabelle said coolly.

"Sure," I said. I had to maintain plausible deniability. "I mean, I only notice it on trans women. It's a tell, sort of. Too perfect. On you, though — " I paused conspicuously " — it could work."

Her smirk stayed fixed in place but her eyebrows raised a little bit.

"Oh, yeah, I know what you're talking about," Dustin said. "'Too perfect' is a good way of putting it. The like, Long Island housewife look."

"Exactly," I said.

"I sort of feel like it's really normal for rich women in New York to get FFS," Dustin said. "Cis women, I mean."

"There's a difference between cosmetic surgery for cis people and facial reconstructive surgery for trans women," Arabelle said coldly.

She was repeating slogans she had seen on Instagram, which meant I was winning. I decided to ignore her.

"I'm from Chicago and we call it *North Shore face*," I said, directing the comment at Dustin. "The FFS surgeon there, I don't even remember his name, I didn't consider him for a second; he's infamous for routinely making his trans patients look like that. It's the same thing."

"It's always, y'know, at risk of sounding insensitive, the white ethnics who do it," Dustin said. "Like the Italians and Eastern Europeans. Like, they don't fit into conventional beauty standards either."

"Right," I agreed. I turned to Arabelle finally. "I don't buy that it's *facial reconstruction*. You just have to say that it's medically necessary for insurance reasons. And, like, you're gonna get a nose job, right?"

"I mean, to be clear, I think getting a nose job is cool," Dustin said. "I would get one."

I had cracked her confidence a little bit. She was looking out into the rainy night, fidgeting with a scrunchie, fidgeting with the zipper on her perfect jacket. She reached up to tie her hair back. She had beautiful hair, long and straight down with a thousand shades of brown and gold in it.

"I don't appreciate the way you're talking to me," she finally said.

Dustin looked up at me with a facial expression I recognized from childhood — the amused gaze of the spectator. I noted that Arabelle didn't direct any of her anger at him.

Now that she had her hair up, and because the topic was her face, I willed myself to look at her with the eyes of a surgeon.

"Once you get surgery," I said, keeping my voice even, "you'll be able to wear your hair in a ponytail like that more often."

"Excuse me?" she said.

"The brow ridge, you know," I said casually, tossing my cigarette butt into the sidewalk. "You won't have to worry about it."

"Alright. I'm going inside," Arabelle said.

"Cool, I'll see you in there," I said.

She wasn't going to give me the satisfaction of untying her hair in front of me, but I was sure she'd do it once she was inside. I wondered if she was gonna run into those Discord transbians. I asked Dustin for another cigarette.

Before he could acknowledge anything about that exchange, I asked him about his novel. It sounded completely conventional and sort of dull. I moved closer to him, and we were both leaning on the railing, side by side, our arms touching.

Eventually, Ambrose opened the door. I had sort of expected to see him.

"Hey V, how's it going?" he said.

"Pretty good," I said. "This is Dustin."

"I know Dustin," he said.

Of course he did.

"Are you trying to leave soon?" Ambrose said.

Dustin placed his hand on my lower back, underneath the scaly top. I didn't disallow the gesture.

"Not really," I said. I leaned into Dustin in a totally unsubtle way. "I'm having a good time catching up with people. Aren't you?"

"I don't know," Ambrose said, looking at the front door with what could have been mild panic. "I guess I'll stay here for longer. I just wanted to check in with you."

"You do that," I said.

"This party sucks," I said, when Ambrose was gone.

"Yeah," Dustin said. "Do you wanna, uh, walk with me a bit? I live just near here."

"Me too," I lied, even though at that point I was pretty certain I didn't need any pretense. "I'll walk with you."

We walked back to his place on the straightest path. The rain got more insistent and then turned into sleet. At one point, I put my arm around his waist, like I would for a woman, and felt him shrink into me. For the first time in weeks, I got a little turned on.

Gap Year

September 10

Genevieve,

Yesterday I went to Elena's house again. She asked me if I knew how you were doing, and I said no. Have you thought about calling her? Ever since she broke her leg, all she has is free time.

September 14

That probably wasn't such a good way to start. You're busy; it's natural. And you live in, like — where do you live now? Far away from here. I see pictures on Instagram and I get confused. There's somehow both mountains and an ocean nearby. Or are you traveling a lot?

People here miss you, though, and everyone seems to think that I'm the best person to ask about how you're doing, and I don't really know. It's been a while. Not too long, but long enough.

September 14 (later)

A month ago, someone you don't talk to anymore told me about you. "If she decides that she doesn't like you, there's nothing you can do," he said. "You'll never see her again."

I was torn. Because, like, yeah, I've seen you do that; but also I couldn't help but think that the difference between you and me is that I was still talking to him. This kind of annoying, emotionally congested French lit major. I had been listening to him reminisce aimlessly for nearly an hour as we chained cigs on a bridge by the river, wondering if this was important. You don't even *live* here anymore.

September 17

I think I used to feel like my life was tending toward some final, unavoidable confrontation. Now I have no ambitions, no plans, nothing that needs to be resolved right away. This is a good place for that feeling. I bet you can imagine what it's like here for me. You would be impatient with all of it, probably. The same parties, the same conversations recur over and over. People tend to outgrow it. Elena's been talking a lot about grad school.

The freight train tracks cross the street next to the Food Co-Op. From the side yard, where I take my smoke breaks, I can see how they cut through Ypsilanti. The warehouses and old brick buildings look haphazardly placed next to it, at strange angles to the straight, flat, purposeful line the train cuts on its way to Detroit, and from there to everywhere else, probably.

September 26

I often think of you when I walk home. Sometimes it feels like I'm always walking home, like that's the only part I ever retain and the rest of it is the daydream.

When I get home my room feels empty, even with me in it. I watch hazy evening light cast shadows in the shape of branches and leaves on the wall opposite my bed. I look around at my possessions. Necessities piled next to things I keep around to help me remember. Photographs pinned to the wall, some telling prints and posters. You can add or subtract, but you can't be on your way anywhere.

October 1

I spent the summer after I turned twenty working at a Kroger's in Grand Rapids, keeping my head down. All I remember from that time was that my day began, most of the time, with a long, sweaty bike ride on the shoulder of a four-lane road.

I was spending a lot of time nervously searching stuff about hormones on the internet. It's funny how much I take it for granted now, because back then, the thought of having to ask a doctor, politely, for estrogen made me so anxious that it threatened to undo the whole thing. Elena suggested to me, over the phone, to wait until I got back to school to think about it.

September rolled around. My mom was slightly incredulous about the shabby mansion, carved into twenty-five little rooms, that I was moving into. People streamed in and out of the narrow front door carrying boxes and suitcases.

"This?" she said, looking across the gearbox at me.

"Yeah," I said.

She hugged me outside and then drove away once I got my two suitcases out of the backseat. Once she was gone, I spotted Elena sitting on the porch, wearing a bandana around her forehead and big sunglasses that covered half her face. When she saw me, she grinned and came down to hug me. I winced a little bit when she used my new name.

Inside, people came and went, putting their rooms together. Murals covered every surface of the walls, months-old flyers corroded on a poster board outside the cavernous kitchen, cardboard signs taped to the wall indicated chore assignments, whose stuff was whose, and how to keep the public spaces clean. The furniture was all second-hand. None of the chairs matched and there were marker drawings and deep scratches all over the long, wide kitchen table. There was, inexplicably, a church pew in the kitchen. Elena told me, after she finished helping me unpack, about the tradition of "hippie Christmas" — apparently, there was a lot of good stuff to be had in the weeks after graduation if one rooted around in the dumpsters behind the houses on Frat Row. Working kitchen appliances, textbooks in original plastic wrappers, houseplants still clinging to life, bags of drugs, mysterious curiosities. The people who spent the summer here would go in the middle of the night, stifling their laughter and shushing each other.

The co-ops were a kind of paradise for the sort of post-adolescent who needs to "figure themselves out" on a large, permissive canvas of potential. I was like that, obviously, but there were extremes I didn't know were possible. Elena and I walked past the open doorway of a guy who had stripped the curtains from the windows and was in the process of painting everything, including the floorboards, solid white. Elena told him it looked like "a temple to the sun" and he didn't get that she was making fun of him.

"Is he just gonna, like, sleep on the couch tonight?" Elena said later. She was sitting on my bed while I hung up posters on the eggplant-purple walls. "It's gonna smell like paint for *days*."

"I guess so."

"God, I'm glad I'm living here this year," she said, brushing a few purple-edged curls out of her face. "You're gonna love it. It's so much less *straight* here."

She had been saying this since she helped me move in, in a sort of refrain. I didn't respond because I was contemplating where to put my trans flag, a gift from my parents. It was... too big. I had to stretch my arms way out to hold it all the way open.

"Hey Elena, is this tacky?" I said, holding up the flag.
"What's that?"
"The trans flag."
"Oh," she said, cocking her head to one side. "Yeah, I wouldn't."

I spent the afternoon and evening setting up my room. When I came downstairs, the living room was lit up by a purple rotating light and my housemates were drinking beers on the couch. I sat in a wicker armchair near them and quietly rolled a joint on a hardback copy of Nietzsche's *The Gay Science* that someone had left on a coffee table. By the time I was done there were more people. After someone started playing music from a Bluetooth speaker, I got up and drifted through the other rooms down to the kitchen, then out onto the porch, and then back to where I had started. People kept arriving.

In my first two years of college, I realized, I'd accumulated a lot of acquaintances but no one I could talk to for more than ten seconds in an environment like this. I'd say hi, and within a moment I would realize that we had exhausted our possible conversation. The groupings that formed on the porch and in the kitchen were opaque. People had formed new alliances over the summer, people were newly dating or broken up, people tried on new personality traits. Elena could parse it, I think. I would catch a glimpse of her laughing in circles full of boys or touching the bare, tattooed arms of girls, a light touch that was an extension of listening to whatever they were saying.

I ended up on the porch, where people were smoking and there was a lessened expectation for conversation. The purple light from the living room fanned out of the front windows in regular pulses. I stared out into the blue darkness of the yard, a hazy orange streetlight glow hovering at the end of it.

This is so stupid, I thought. And then, *I need to think. When will I have time to think?*

People filtered away, and eventually the only person left was a girl wearing a pastel pink hoodie and some complicated-looking skirt, puffing on the end of a cigarette and looking vacantly out into space. That was you.

"Hey," you said as I approached.

"Hey," I said back.

"Is that a joint?" you asked.

"Yeah," I said.

"Are you trans?" you said.

"Yeah," I managed.

"Cool, me too. I'm Genevieve. Can I have some of your weed?"

"Yeah, could I have one of your cigs?"

You pushed the pink hood off your head and shook out a tangle of brownish hair with a bit of pink at the ends. I noticed that there was, like, a lot of glitter on your face. Maybe too much. It made your face look pale and fragile. In every other respect you looked like a teenager, awkward and ill-at-ease in your own body, hunching over, shifting your weight a lot.

Music from the house filtered through the quickening dusk. We passed the joint quickly back and forth. We found out that we lived within two blocks of each other and that we were both English majors. Then some guys came out of the house with beer, and someone you knew pulled you away. I ended up saying hi to someone I had classes with last year.

He struggled to remember me. "Oh, we were in — what was it?"

"Chaucer," I said.

"Oh, riiiiight," he said.

I just nodded. Then he had some question about me — how was your summer, what are you taking this term, blah blah blah — and as I answered automatically I zoned out and my ambient thoughts started playing on loop, like a screensaver: *Does this guy know I'm trans? Is he treating me differently? Talking to me as an equal or talking down to me? Is he enlightened, chauvinistic, what difference does that make? Do I ever really get treated like a woman or just like some other third thing halfway between a wimpy guy and a null pointer? Is there any way to tell about any of this?* Then, in counterpoint, the self-aware layer: *He doesn't care that you're trans, you care that you're trans; you're staring at your shoes all the time expecting everyone else to be staring too.*

I realized that I was too stoned for this conversation and should probably go upstairs, but I wanted to talk to you again. Unsure how to escape, I stared into the face of the Chaucer guy as he talked about Sartre or Heidegger or northern Michigan or his girlfriend's parents or which co-ops throw good parties or snowboarding or whatever else passed for conversation in the rich suburb of Detroit that he was probably from. I kept wondering what I would say to you next, but at some point I looked up and you were gone.

October 3

When classes started, Elena and I resumed a version of the routine we had in the dorms — after dinner, we would sit in the armchairs in the living room or go to the library until our eyes hurt from the fluorescent ceiling lights.

"Do you know someone named Genevieve?" I said to her one day as we were walking back at one in the morning.

"Yeah, doesn't she live at Vail House?" she said. "You're both trans," she added.

"Yeah, her," I said. "I think I have a crush on her."

"Oh. Hmm. Good luck with that," she said.

"What does that mean?"

She seemed to think. "Someone told me that she's actively not dating right now," she said. "Also, maybe she's straight."

"That's fine," I said. "It's just a crush. I don't know if I'm going to do anything about it."

"Mm," Elena said, sounding unconvinced and uninterested.

Elena always had crushes for good reasons, usually on a close female friend whose intelligence or worldliness she admired and envied. She seemed to think that a crush was a humiliating downgrade from friendship, and out of a sense of respect she would try to stifle her feelings in a way that really just fermented the crush in silent, tortured yearning. Sometimes it would fade, but other times she would end up confessing recursively complicated feelings in a teary rush after some late night of drinking and long conversations. Sometimes her feverish desires were returned and would have to be painfully brought down to a normal level, and sometimes friendships were broken off or left ragged, and she'd cry bitterly about it and move on.

Asking her for advice seemed impossible because she lived in a world where women constructed grand narratives out of their lives, and I didn't. I figured at some point, if transitioning worked like everyone on the internet said it did, my life would resemble Elena's more. At the moment, though, people always seemed to glance off me like drops of water.

This was a different sort of crush, my first as a woman. It felt important in a way that seems funny in retrospect. I found myself half-expecting you everywhere. I would be standing in the kitchen making coffee, and I'd hear someone shuffling down the stairs and find myself hoping it was you, with some improbable reason to be at my house at seven in the morning. But then what? *Oh, yeah, we met. Bye.* It was never you, though.

October 5

Maybe I was expecting to run into you because we followed each other on social media, which you used like a diary. On Tumblr you reblogged pictures of high fashion, quoted Donna Haraway and Julia Serano, and took sides in incomprehensible arguments about gender. On Instagram you posted pictures where your face was obscured and documented your friends endlessly. It was like the divide between your inner and outer life.

I noticed that you were a member of a small friend group who played in bands together. Your pictures made it seem like there was always something going on in some living room, some kitchen, some backyard. You started commenting on my posts and it felt a little like we were becoming acquainted.

Isn't it hard to talk about the parts of our lives we live online? It somehow always comes across more superficial than it actually is. One day, you DM'd me: *Hey, wanna hang out?* The simplicity of it disarmed me enough that what I said in response was *of course*.

October 7

We met in front of your house. It was lightly drizzling, one of the first cool autumn days. You came out wearing sunglasses, even though it was overcast. Your hair was longer. That made me feel better, because as nervous as I was about talking to you again, it was nice to be reminded that we were both growing our hair out, and probably doing a bunch of other things at around the same time and for the same reasons.

You chose a direction. We walked down State Street making small talk. *How've you been? Tired. Already? Yeah.* By the time we wound up in the cheap coffee shop that the graduate students like, I liked you and you had become a real person to me.

You ordered a big pot of green tea. I found out that you were from upstate New York and that you grew up playing pond hockey before going to an all-boys boarding school.

"That sucked," you said, and then changed the subject.

I got the sense of a life full of difficulties. Later, you told me, almost in passing, that your dad had been really awful to you when you were a teenager. You didn't give details, and I didn't ask for them.

"It's fine, though," you said. "I don't want you to think that I'm, like, in grave danger. I'm not even really dependent on him anymore."

"Isn't he paying your tuition?"

"It's complicated," you said.

When we hit snags like that, you'd ask me about myself. I answered your questions, sometimes long-windedly, never quite believing what I was saying. You were a good listener, and I wished that you weren't, because I didn't have my own biography in order yet, and I wasn't sure what bits to emphasize and which to let fade into silence beyond reminiscence. It felt like the longer I talked, the more I got lost.

When I got back, it was totally dark. Elena was sprawled on a couch reading *Madame Bovary*.

"How'd it go?" she called out as I climbed the stairs.

"Fine," I said, trying to make it sound as though I had downgraded my crush to the appropriate level. "She's cool, you know?"

Elena gave me a quizzical smile, as though there was some joke I wasn't in on yet.

October 9

Sometime in October I was on a break from my structuralism seminar, eating a candy bar in the hallway. There were maybe fifteen kids just milling around in the space outside the lecture hall, texting while leaning against concrete pillars, some reading the textbook, some doing homework for other classes already. When I saw you on the other side of the hallway, you smiled and shuffled over to where I was standing.

"Hey," I said.

You started rifling through your backpack. "Wanna walk to the Dana building with me? I need to turn in some forms."

"Sure."

I sat outside an office door while I listened to you try to explain something to someone in a position of authority. It dragged on until the second half of my seminar was over, so I had to run to get my laptop out of the room after everyone else had shuffled out. The TA gave me a long, sad look from where he was putting papers back into his worn leather shoulder bag.

Another time, my house threw a party and I saw you in the kitchen wearing a lot of black mesh and pleather. You were really drunk and put both of your hands on my shoulders and said: "Oh my *godddd*. My *faaaavorite* girl is here." I felt a weightless rush, giddily excited in a way raised to vaudeville proportions by the amount of alcohol I had consumed, and I put my hands on your waist and giggled wordlessly as you drew me into a hug. I felt like we might lose balance and fall over. Then someone in the other room was crying and you had to intervene.

A week or two later I was doing my homework in the co-op living room and you walked through with two guys, clearly the ringleader. You were wearing a sort of black denim shirt, unbuttoned to your sternum, tucked into a pleated plaid skirt that looked like it was snipped and sewed from a grandmother's tablecloth. You were wearing fishnets and big black boots.

Outside, the wind was stripping brown-and-red leaves from the trees. The guys looked so plain next to you. I looked up and waved, and you smiled and waved back.

October 15

At a quiet weeknight party, I kissed a girl named Kira. She had been very purposefully flirty with me all night — lots of eye contact, very attentive listening as I talked, always finding excuses to keep the conversation going, talking a lot about her feelings. She had a big mane of curly, dark hair and a perpetually flushed face. "You're *so* pretty," she said. I kissed her back but sort of stumbled away before her roving hands could unmask the body I was hiding underneath a baggy sweatshirt and jeans. I ended up on the porch, fiddling around in my jacket pockets to find a cigarette. Elena was out there, smoking and looking at her phone, perched on a handrail.

"I think I really need to get on estrogen," I said.

Elena looked up and looked at me strangely. "Do it, then," she said firmly, but without a trace of anger, looking right at me. She returned to her phone, typing something rapidly.

Just then Kira came outside, and without speaking she walked over to Elena and sat on the handrail next to her. I walked over to the other side of the porch and pretended they weren't there and finished my cigarette, staring at the wet leaf litter. I looked at Kira and she was looking at me with a sort of sad, curious expression. She didn't mean me any harm. I forced a smile. I was grateful when she looked away.

October 20

A day later Kira texted me. Elena had given her my number. *I totally understand if I misread your intentions*, she said. *You don't talk much. But I like you and would be happy if I could see you again.*

Elena had some inclination toward playing matchmaker with her friends. My mom, who knew her growing up, once said that Elena was a "meddler." It was a relief, as someone who was chronically uninvolved, to be around someone like that.

I rashly invited Kira to a Halloween party at one of the co-op houses. Later that week I came downstairs one day and she was sitting with a group of her friends in the corner, doing homework. I said her name once and she looked up, gave a faint smile and a slight wave, and then looked back down at her laptop. One of her friends next to her, who had red hair and big glasses, looked up too, and her eyes were on me for a little longer, appraising.

The day of the party I was in my room putting on a sort of half-assed costume — I don't even remember what it was — when there was a knock on my door. Before I could say anything, Kira poked her head in. She was wearing a sort of leotard thing and big bunny ears.

"Hi," I said.

"Hey."

She hugged me and then, seemingly impulsively, she gave me a little kiss on the side of my neck, where my hair was held away in a ponytail.

That was what did it. Whatever part of me had tensed before with her relaxed, and before we had said two words to each other she was on top of me on my floor, holding my hands behind my head and furiously working her hips. When she shuddered and convulsed on top of me I was briefly not there, and then I was back, staring at my ceiling, the zipper of something I had left on the floor digging into my ass. The whole scene had acquired a sort of sordid quality, not appealing at all.

"Jesus," she groaned in my ear.

We didn't talk much on the way to the party. Somehow we kept running into people we wanted to talk to — in the hallways of my house, on the porch of the house the party was at. Talking to other people provided a good way to avoid talking to each other. Every so often she would put her hand around my nonexistent waist or sort of stroke my hair, as if to remind me. We had never really had a conversation and it was like she owned me. I tried to decide if I liked it.

I think I had too much on my mind to have fun at the party, but I ended up drinking a lot, in a way that doesn't furnish funny stories later. I fell down on the porch when a guy wearing a fat suit shoved me, then I threw up in some bushes on my way home. It was the first time I had thrown up from drinking.

"Did it make you, like, dysphoric?" Elena asked later.

"No," I said. "What does that even mean? It felt normal, I think."

"You're hard to read," Elena complained.

"I think I was hoping that we would have more in common," I said.

"Sure," Elena said. "Sorry, I don't need to make everything a trans thing."

"It's okay," I said.

November 1

Like, obviously I was dysphoric. I don't remember feeling anguished or upset in the moment, it just nags at me retrospectively. I remember thinking, *It might as well be this. It's just as likely as anything else, probably.*

Dysphoria is a scary word, and for a long time I thought it was reserved for emotions adjacent to desperation, madness, disintegration — I read once about a trans woman back in the day who cut her own junk off when she got denied for surgery. Now I think that maybe the thing with dysphoria is that it doesn't begin or end anywhere in particular. I wonder about that woman —I could see myself doing something like that if I was less afraid of pain, if only to force this fine mist of vague unease to coalesce on something, like holding a magnet up to metal shavings. Does the magnet reveal the true nature of the metal, or just one of the properties it happens to have?

I think the biggest thing that bugged me about Kira was that she seemed so free, so sure in what she wanted. I didn't know at all. When I ran into her in the living room again, we smiled and waved to each other, but that was it. Later we became friends and never mentioned what happened between us.

November 12

What else?

I went on estrogen, and for about a month I was convinced it didn't do anything. Then — you know. That feeling like a big, cumbersome part of you that you had been dragging around your whole life just goes to sleep. It was strange.

I joined the lit mag, which was sort of a joke, but they did publish a story I wrote. It's about a trans girl at college, you know, the thing all my stories were about. She experiences, like, microaggressions and feels bad about it. Regrettable, but what did I know? It's not even like that was my life. People mostly just ignored me. When they spoke, they got it right. If they didn't, they'd say sorry.

Maybe I was looking for a way to externalize some of my angst. At the time, I was so convinced that everyone could clearly see my inner confusion, and probably that you could see it more than anyone. In reality everyone was so wrapped up in their own shit that both of us barely registered as a problem to solve or an incongruity to understand, and I pretended to find my own increasingly visible gender issues more or less uninteresting, not worth talking about.

I wonder sometimes if you felt as lost amid all this as I did, and whether you had the same kind of tentative curiosity about me that I did about you. And I guess I wonder if you were really like me, or if we both just ended up in the same place.

November 28

I saw you again on the roof of Angell Hall after it had gotten really cold. It was the astronomy club open house. I was with a ragtag group of co-op boys who quickly wanted to get under the dome of the telescope. I walked over to the edge of the roof, looking down onto the snow-covered Diag.

You startled me by coming up behind me and saying, "Hi there, girl." I spun around and hugged you in your big blue winter coat and smelled whisky on your breath.

Via Instagram I knew you had started a band, so I had something to talk to you about. "It's going okay," you said. "I've, like, played in bands before, but this is the first group I've really, like, musically vibed with, you know?"

I noticed there was a guy standing slightly behind you, grad student-y in a black peacoat and blue jeans, drinking from a flask and scrutinizing me, not shivering at all. I nodded to him.

"This is Jonas," you said.

"Pleasure," he said stiffly.

"Jesus, dude, how the fuck have you been doing," you said, slurring your words slightly. "Jonesie. Can we have a minute?" To this Jonas just nodded and we drifted away from him toward the telescope. You grabbed my hand and pulled me along, talking rapidly.

The observatory was mostly just an open-air section of the roof with a couple picnic tables held down with sandbags and chains. Toward the middle of it, there was a bisected dome that had a long, imposing telescope poking out. I expected the pink hair when you took off your hood, but you had cut it short and it was black.

"It sounds like you're doing really well," you said, after I had tried to summarize things. "You know, considering everything. I feel like it's been a really weird year for everyone."

I nodded. We had ended up next to the eyepiece, where a group of hardcore science kids were discussing something with the professor, who looked like Santa Claus. You were still holding on to my hand, and you had one fingertip making a little circle in the fleshy part of my palm.

"I read your story," you said. "I liked it a lot."

"Thank you," I said, and pulled my hand away.

"Hey ladies," the professor said from over the heads of the swarm of undergrads. "Wanna take a look?"

You bent down to stick your face in the eyepiece. I looked up at the long metal tube sticking into the ceiling of the dome, with a ring of softly glowing night sky around it.

"What am I looking at?" you said.

"The Pleiades," said one of the undergrads.

"The Seven Sisters," the professor said sonorously.

Jonas drifted over and said something about getting going, that he was freezing up here.

"Jonesie, you are *so* much trouble," you said in an exaggerated falsetto, not looking up from the eyepiece.

"Excuse me?"

You switched your voice from Valley girl to Betty Boop. "You *heard* me. I'm *trying* to look at the *stars*, you know, the whole reason we *came* here?"

"Okay," he said testily.

"I'm starting to think you're no good for me," you said.

"Jesus," he muttered. "You're trashed. Can we talk about this somewhere else?"

"Jonesie. The *stars*," you said, louder and higher-pitched.

"Stop calling me that," he said quietly. He was clearly trying to avoid drawing attention to himself.

"Okay. Jonas. I'm looking at the *stars*, so I guess you'll have to go suck your own dick tonight."

"Alright, if you're gonna be like that — " he made a move to grab your arm but one of the science kids — a six-foot-three guy with a jaw like a shovel — got between you and Jonas and shoulder-checked him lightly.

"Hey, you heard him," he said, laughing. "Your boyfriend wants to look at the stars. If you're cold, the door is that way, *Jonesie*." Even the professor was laughing.

After he stormed off you stood up and offered me the eyepiece.

"Wanna look?" you said.

I looked. I couldn't see anything.

"He taught a philosophy class I was in as a freshman," you said. "He's like, twenty-six." This was fifteen minutes later, as we were walking down Washtenaw toward our neighborhood. You had sobered up quickly.

"Ew."

"Don't 'ew' me," you said incredulously. "I'm already judging myself enough about this."

I apologized.

Even though we hadn't talked very much since the time we went to the coffee shop together, it was easy to talk to you. When we got back to my house we stood facing each other expectantly on the front porch stairs. I studied your nearly bald head, your goofy smile, and I nervously pushed a strand of hair behind my ears, stuffed both my hands into my jacket pockets.

"Can I kiss you?" I said.

When you looked back at me, the amber glow of the streetlights had washed all the green out of your eyes. You closed your mouth, but you were still smiling. Then you looked down at your shoes and took a shuffling step backward.

"No," you said carefully. "I'm sorry, I just — "

"It's okay," I said, with what I hoped was finality. You smiled and hugged me tightly, like before but more briefly, and I went inside.

January 1

When you apologized for being drunk and making a scene on the rooftop a couple days later, I was a little sad that you never mentioned the moment on my steps, but I understood. I knew that you knew how much I was infatuated with you, and I took it as a compliment that you still wanted to be my friend enough to apologize to me when you didn't need to.

You stood in the doorway to my room while you said your piece. I was reading *The Second Sex* for a class, wearing two sweaters underneath the covers in my bed. I told you to come in, and you told me to come to the library with you.

"I have a paper due tomorrow," you said. "I'll probably be there for a while. I just didn't want to be alone."

It was the Saturday of the winter study break. Everything was covered in a strange purple glow that descended from the overcast sky and made warped shadows on the snowbanks. We climbed the wide steps to the huge, glowing library in silence.

We eventually came upon a forgotten corner, deep in the stacks, far away from any sign of life. The rows of books veered off into infinite space under the buzzing fluorescent lights. Against a bare wall, two green, scrolled armchairs sat next to each other with a little circular table in between them. It looked like a corner of a house where a married couple reads the newspaper every night.

I sat next to you and got absorbed in my book, deep into the night. You typed and typed and typed. The Second Sex became impossible to read at around six in the morning, so I wandered off into the stacks and looked for something else. I returned with Bibliography of Ancient Sumerian Religion and spent an hour or so letting the titles of conference papers and dissertations slip past my eyes. At some point, you finished typing, slammed your laptop closed, and grinned at me.

On the way back, we talked about everything we still had to do, and you told me that you were also staying for winter break. Back at the co-op, we sat together as my housemates came in and out, you poking at your phone and drinking black coffee out of a Moscow mule mug, me just sort of staring off into space. We blended back into the morning scene, when we had been outside of time for a little while. People said hi to you, and you talked and talked and talked.

January 10

We were friends after that. One day over winter break, I came back from a long, aimless walk and found you and a group of guys I knew in the living room with a drum set and some amplifiers. When I walked in, everyone started laughing.

"Um, hi," you said. "We're rehearsing."

"Something like that," the drummer said.

You started up again, once I was in my room. Covers of the Cranberries and Fiona Apple and some stuff I didn't recognize. Afterward, you knocked on my door.

"Hey, sorry if that was too loud. Can I hang in here for a sec?"

"Sure."

"I'm overstimulated. This is, like, the chill out room."

I had painted the walls a deep russet red and strung up a bunch of Christmas lights. You plopped yourself into my chair.

This became a regular thing once classes started. Most evenings we would read in the same room or do homework. Other times you'd pick out tunes on your guitar. We spent a lot of time like that, sometimes not talking, sometimes talking a lot.

One of the things that fascinated me about you was your air of preoccupation when you were thinking. If there was some idea that wouldn't come, you'd sit there and stare just past your laptop screen until you thought of it. When you were playing guitar, you'd play the same phrases over and over, changing one or two notes, until you liked it enough to continue. Everything was getting worked out thoroughly in your head.

Once, late at night, while I was catching up on something, you were laying in my bed. Without saying anything, you handed me your phone.

"What do you think of this guy?"

It was a picture of a dude wearing the same university sweatshirt that everyone who didn't know how to dress could fall back on. I swiped on his profile and saw a picture of a modestly built torso taken in a bathroom with the flash on.

"Is this Grindr?"

"Yeah. I just downloaded it on a whim. This is the first guy who tapped me."

I realized at that point that, despite mounting evidence to the contrary, I had sort of been assuming you were a lesbian, like me. Jonesie couldn't convince me otherwise, but this could. This wasn't an idea that you were trying to talk yourself into, you were actually considering the guy in the sweatshirt. I let myself feel slightly superior to you for a moment.

"I'm the wrong person to ask," I said, handing the phone back.

January 25

Even so, when you told me about James I thought it was a joke.

"Is he from Grindr?" I asked.

"No, he's someone I knew from when I was ten years old."
"Does *he* know that?"
"Be serious."

Elena and I both wanted to meet your new boyfriend, and what you suggested was, for some odd reason, going to the arboretum after a huge snowstorm at the end of January. James showed up in full skiing regalia — snow pants, a hat with ear flaps, the works — and Elena and I were wearing, like, jeans.

I immediately liked him. Obviously, I thought you were superior to him in every way. He was confident and in shape but not beautiful, and you could talk circles around him, and frequently interrupted him. He seemed to admire you in a dopey sort of way, and only once or twice did it cross my mind that you and him had been teenage boys together.

You tried to convince us to walk across the frozen river. I got too scared to get far from the shore, so Elena and I hung back while you and James shuffled out there.

"C'mon over!" you shouted from the opposite riverbank.

"Fuck off!" Elena yelled back, grinning.

"I weigh, like, twice as much as either of you," James shouted.

"They're like faggot high school sweethearts," Elena said to me while we were finding another way to cross the river. "They're either going to kill each other or get married."

At the one show that your band played, I hung around while you socialized with the other musicians and a few of James's friends, and I was surprised at how well you did with them. I never did very well in open-ended conversations with straight engineering students from Grosse Pointe, but you were hitting all the beats, feigning interest in things. I stood in that circle saying nothing and then retreated to the back with Elena and Kira while you went to set up.

It was in the rearranged living room of one of the co-ops, and you were performing in the kitchen. Someone turned off all the lights but the overhead in the kitchen, and then, when people still wouldn't shut up, you just started playing. I had heard you play this riff much slower in my bedroom, and just like in my bedroom, you stared down at your guitar while you played. Even though you barely looked up from the fretboard, I could tell from your tight-lipped grin that you were having a great time, loved all the attention you were getting.

Elena and I both agreed later that it was impossible to tell what you were singing, except for the covers. The sound balance was completely wrong, and the guitars and drums drowned out your voice almost completely. After the show James gave you flowers, and, yes, I felt a little jealous of him, but not very much at that point. Elena saw me watching you standing with him in the doorway and elbowed me hard in the side.

February 20

By then Elena had coupled up with Kira. One night in Elena's bedroom after a party I was talking to you and the drummer in your band, and across the room the two of them began shamelessly making out on Elena's bed. The drummer kept talking about Thomas Pynchon as if nothing was happening.

"Finally," you mouthed at me.

Sometime in February Kira and Elena invited you, James, and I to a house Kira's parents owned in Muskegon, right on Lake Michigan, for spring break.

"I hope you won't feel like a perpetual third wheel," you said offhandedly a week beforehand. I hadn't even considered it. Being a third wheel felt like one of those fake emotional states left over from high school.

But when I got there, and unpacked everything in the wood-paneled bedroom on the first floor, I did start to feel a little lonely. Enough clothes for the week and a big stack of books, all in a pile on an old blue quilt. On the wall there was a painting of a sailing ship and an embroidery piece with a Bible verse on it. A mirror above the dresser. I adjusted my hair in it.

I didn't want a lover, I wanted someone I could talk to, and I had that in you. But the bed with the blue quilt looked forbiddingly cold.

All week it was overcast and fifty degrees. The house was surrounded by brambly, gray woods. We did homework around the big, empty house and went on walks by the shore. I spent most of my time on the back deck, trying to write a story for my fiction class and chain-smoking. Elena would come chat with me or offer me tea, then she'd go back inside to where Kira was sitting next to the fireplace puzzling over physics equations. At night, two or three of us would cook dinner and you would pick out chords on the deck or sing songs with Kira while the rest of us read inside. At night I opened the window so the lake would partially drown out the sound of Elena and Kira having sex.

The fiction class was my main source of vexation that semester. Trying to create characters on the page while the characters in front of me all crowded out my ability to think clearly. I started to think that it was stupid to encourage people my age to write. I should have been like you — you can write good songs when you're twenty-one, because songs are just feelings. Feelings were really all I had.

I woke up the day before we left and realized that I was nearly a week late on my estrogen shot. In the kitchen, I asked you if you brought yours and you said yes, go ahead.

When I drew it up in the bathroom, I realized I just couldn't do it. Something in me was preventing me from sticking the needle in my thigh, like I had maybe two dozen times before. I stared at it, willing myself to muster up the courage, and it didn't come.

"Hey, we're going on a walk," Kira said through the door, maybe fifteen minutes into this ordeal. "Do you wanna come?"

"No," I said. The screen door banged.

I sat there for maybe half an hour. I came close to calling you, asking you to come back and do it for me, but I didn't. I eventually gave up and just sat there, holding the syringe outward from me, vibrating with anxiety and self-pity.

When I heard the screen door open, I briefly tried again, but couldn't get myself to do it. I finally just pulled my pants back up and walked out into the kitchen, where you were chopping something.

"Hey Gen?" I asked. I realized there was a little bit of crying in my voice.

"Are you okay?"

"Yeah, uh, can you do my shot for me?"

Your eyes widened a bit. You held the knife out from your body like you weren't sure what to do with it.

"I'm in the middle of this," you finally said. "But, uh — James?"

He was leaning on the counter, looking at his phone. He looked up.

"Can you do her shot for her?"

"Oh, sure," he said.

"Would that be okay?" you said, looking at me with a strained expression.

I was in no place to refuse. We shuffled back to the bathroom together and he knelt in front of me.

"I do this for Genevieve," he said.

His voice was soft and firm, fatherly. I looked down at his face. It didn't have a trace of pity on it, but it was kind. I handed him the syringe.

He did it, quickly and painlessly. By the end of it I wasn't crying anymore. He capped the syringe and patted me on the side of my thigh before going back out into the kitchen.

I dried my face on the towel and walked out past you. You looked at me with an expression of mild concern, but I got to the screen door and quickly left before you could say anything.

I walked to the beach, because there was nowhere else to go. The humiliation was wearing off. I was glad, in the end, that you weren't the one who did it. Without really thinking what I was doing, I walked into the water, fully clothed. It was freezing cold. I kept walking. When water reached my waist, I stopped.

I had the realization that not even a year ago I would have been tempted to keep going as far as I could, maybe until I froze or drowned, and now, I had no interest in that. I could already feel the power of the waves, could see how easily I could just get ripped away out into it. The lake was beautiful. You could tell that it barely noticed you as you stared out into it, and I liked that.

March 1

Maybe my memories have less to teach me than I originally thought. I've decided that when I'm done writing whatever this is, I'm going to burn it, and then I'm going to call you.

May 7

The rest of the semester passed quickly. After graduation, you went with James back to Rochester to see your family immediately, and I stayed where I was. Then you were in Brooklyn, and then Philadelphia. You started another band.

You know this part pretty well, I think, from when we talked on the phone every month or so. I did my last two semesters of school, I fell in love, I moved. I read a lot about religion, which didn't help, and a little bit about meditation, which sort of did. I finished my senior thesis two months after I realized I never wanted to write anything ever again. Gradually, we talked less and less often until it tapered off entirely.

Then, last summer, I was visiting with my friend Taylor, who had just come back from New England. We spent a long afternoon walking around and amicably bickering about philosophy and talking endlessly about the future, going from the carillon tower all the way down to the river and back up, and then it was evening. When we went up to his screened-in porch, you were sitting there, wearing, like, a kimono, reading an old paperback and smoking. You had stopped dyeing your hair different colors and it was just brown and in a shoulder-length bob, the same as mine.

"Oh my god," you said, standing up. You wrapped your arms around my shoulders and giggled a little before sitting down and beckoning me to join you on the chair next to you. Taylor sat down with us but went inside after a few minutes and never came back out. You hardly stopped talking or smoking. I could barely follow it. I kept asking you questions and you kept telling stories.

I wondered if you were ever able to connect your rough, complicated childhood to your headstrong ambition now. Listening to you list the names of musicians, talk about cities I had only ever seen on TV, and talk about boyfriends and hookups and flings, I realized that you had no need to get your life in order. What was past was not prologue, it was a springboard, evaluated for its usefulness and then discarded. I was certain, at that point, that you would end up famous, or, barring that, you would make yourself an interesting life.

At one point, I looked over my shoulder through the window at Taylor's house. The living room had been turned into an impromptu recording studio with a big mixing desk on one side of it and a drum kit on the other. A viney plant grew down from a set of built-in bookshelves.

"Oh, I'm recording some songs, finally," you said.

"How's that?" I said.

"I'm getting there," you said, pursing your lips and flicking your cigarette, looking down at the ground. You were lost in thought again, getting further and further away from me until I couldn't reach you at all. I could have listened to you talk all night, but by midnight I had to go home so I could wake up early for work.

June 1

I haven't seen you since then, but for some reason I'm sure I haven't seen the last of you. You post less and less on the internet, which I always take as a good sign.

For a long time I didn't think about you very much. I was too busy being in love or worrying about myself or, later, trying to be at peace. I had an unremarkable time in college and you were really the only bright spot.

Maybe what I was trying to capture in these pages was your sense of purpose, the way you seemed to cut a straight, clear path through the world. I found myself missing you because I was certain you never lost your sense of direction. There were so many times when something you'd say to me, or just the mere fact of your presence, would make me feel like everything extraneous had fallen away and I lived suddenly in a clean, clear reality that seemed navigable. Those moments are rarer now.

I think once I get that feeling back, I'm going to pack up this bedroom and get a long ways away from here and forget all about it, just like you did.

Now that I've written all of this out, I feel like I've regained some perspective. In a weird way, I don't think it ended up having much to do with you. The plan is still to burn this. Maybe I'll do it tomorrow.

2021-2023

Thank You

Steve, Sara Jane, Verity, Dayton, Maddie, John, Sofia, Jane, Grey, Hazel, Bonnie, Leena, Lily, Clay, Justine, Gigi, Isabel, Evelyn, Eleanor, Esti, Agnes, Eve, Sibyl, Natalie, Ella, Mapes, Meredith, Mallory, Katie Lane, Leah, Kyle, Jackie, Aurora, and Violet.

And especially: Casey and Cat, Mom, Dad, Amory, Sara, and Hannah most of all.

About the Author

Emily Zhou was born in Michigan and lives in New York City. This is her first book.

About LittlePuss Press

LittlePuss Press is a feminist press run by two trans women, Cat Fitzpatrick and Casey Plett. We believe in printing on paper, intensive editing, and throwing lots of parties.

This book is set in Rialto dF, a font designed by calligrapher Giovanni De Faccio and type designer Lui Karner for the C-A-S-T co-operative type foundry. Rialto combines elements from their respective disciplines into a harmonious and lucid whole.